THE HEART IN THE ABBEY

Jane Gregor

Castlepoint

ISBN 978 1897 604 319

Published for the Author by CPP
Kirkcudbrightshire

Cover design by Lisa Neat

Printed in Great Britain by
CPI Antony Rowe

DEDICATION

To my daughter with love and gratitude.
Without her encouragement this book would never
have been finished.

ABOUT THE AUTHOR

In her youth Jane Gregor worked as a sub-editor
for Harpers Bazaar, and contributed articles to
Woman's Hour on the BBC. Now an
octogenarian, she lives in Scotland and this is her
first novel.

Historical Note

'Dulce Cor' - Is Latin for 'Sweet Heart'.

This is a Scottish love story based on historical facts.

It does not claim to be a strictly accurate account of the turbulent thirteenth century times in Great Britain, as ancient records can conflict.

What this book does do is to bring to life historical events.

The chief characters really lived.

The great events they lived through, did indeed happen.

These people, seemingly so far-off and long ago, quarrelled, intrigued, fought and loved as passionately as we do today.

They were people of high rank, intense emotions and their landmarks still exist: Balliol College, Dervorgilla Bridge, Sweetheart Abbey.

Above all, this is a real life love story of which Scotland can be truly proud ... eternally proud.

GLOSSARY

Chapter One

Hodden	Rough grey woollen material
Still-room	Where herbs were hung to dry and distilled, and potions, creams and salves were made up.
Resin lamp	Oil lamp
Sconces	Wall torches
Trencher	Wooden platter with a hollow ring to catch meat juices
Solar	Parlour (talking) room
Pelisse	Long gown/cloak, often fur-lined.
Botel	Ancient name for Buittle Castle, near Dalbeattie.
Filet	Hair net to gather up long hair

Chapter Two

Cambric	Thin cotton material
Castellan	Castle Official
Chaplets	Head garland/wreaths – usually flowers
Tussie-Mussies	Mixed posies of scented flowers
Destriers	Horses
Lumpkin	Rough soldier
Pike	Long pole with one sharp end
Garde-robe	Lavatory

Other Chapters

Hoasts	Coughs
Senechal	Chief Official
Serfs	Peasants

CHRONOLOGY

1213   Dervorgilla is born at Kenmure Castle, Galloway.

1233   Dervorgilla marries Baron John de Balliol.

1251   Bishop of Durham chastises John de Balliol.

1262   Founding of Balliol College at Oxford.

1269   John de Balliol dies in France.
He is embalmed in an ivory casket, banded with silver. This "Sweet Silent Companion" is with Dervorgilla constantly.

1273   Founding of Sweetheart Abbey, Kinderloch.

1282   Dervorgilla grants Charter to Balliol College.

1289   Death of Dervorgilla.
She is buried at Sweetheart Abbey with her "Sweet Silent Companion" laid to rest on top of her heart.

1292–
1296   John, Dervorgilla's son is King of Scotland.

PRESENT DAY

Dervorgilla Bridge is a red sandstone bridge across the River Nith near a weir, now limited to pedestrians.
Balliol College, Oxford, still says a bidding prayer to benefactors John Balliol and his wife Dervorgilla.
Sweetheart Abbey is located in the village of New Abbey, Galloway, Scotland, where the burial site of Dervorgilla and her "Sweet, Silent Companion" can still be seen today.

PRINCIPAL CHARACTERS

Dervorgilla   "Princess" of Galloway, South
                         West Scotland.
John de Balliol   Baron of Picardy origins, with
                         lands in Durham.
                         Signatory of the Magna Carta,
                         Regent of Scotland.
Lord Alan   Dervorgilla's father and
                         Overlord of Galloway.
                         Sometimes referred to as
                         "Prince" Alan.
Christian   Dervorgilla's sister.
William de Fortibus Christian's husband.
Thomas the Bastard   Dervorgilla's half brother,
                         illegitimate son of Lord Alan.
Hugh   Dervorgilla's eldest son.
Alexander   Dervorgilla's second son.
John   Dervorgilla's youngest son
                         and last child.
                         Became King of Scotland
                         1292–1296.

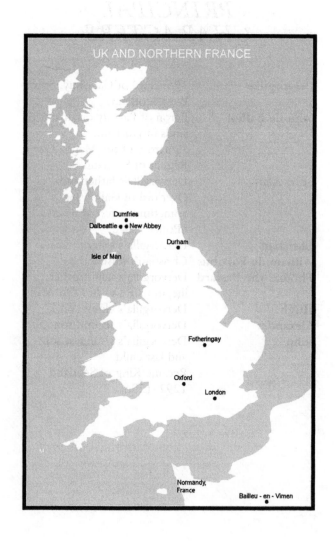

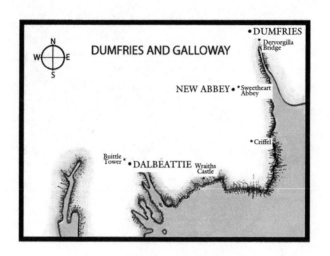

Chapter One

"The marriage settlements have already been sealed. I cannot stop the wedding now!"

Alan, Lord of Galloway drew his fox-lined surcoat closer to him. It was draughty. Would the masons never finish fitting this new glass in the chamber windows of Kenmure? A man needed some protection from the elements if he was not to live like the bog-peasants. Impatiently, he strode the dry rushes of the stone-floored room.

The fair, slender girl who stood before him, biting her lip in order not to cry like a common serving maid, watched him with unhappy eyes.

"But father, he is so much older than I," she ventured "and, they say he's a ..." she coloured ... "a lusty man."

"God's bones," Lord Alan replied, "you're pious enough for two. De Balliol's a powerful man with lands both in England and France. It would be prudent for Galloway to join his lands to ours and marriage is the strongest cement for such a bond."

The girl looked despairingly through the narrow slit of wall which opened to the pale December day beyond the castle walls.

"But I'd rather stay with you. I could go on helping you."

Lord Alan looked sad for a moment. He rose, stiffly, his old wound troubling him in the damp winter air. He laid his hand on his daughter's shoulder.

"You should have been my son." He sighed. "Thomas, even were he lawfully heir, could never ..." He broke off as Dervorgilla interrupted.

"Could you not let Christian marry this Norman knight?" Her father smiled.

"Nay, chick. You know she is promised to William de Fortibus the son of Lord Albermarle."

"I know I may not flout you," the girl answered at length, her green eyes smiling a little before darkening "but may I not plead with you? I scarce know this knight and ... and ..." she faltered "I do not ... love ... him."

"Love? What rubbish is this I hear?" broke in a new voice as a short, plump, high-coloured woman bustled into the room. She seated herself on a chair and began to sew at the woollen embroidery which a young maidservant handed to her.

"Dervorgilla refuses the match I have arranged for her with John de Balliol" her father said.

"Nay, father, refuse I may not," a tiny smile lightened Dervorgilla's expression as she took her father's hand and held it to her cheek.

"I should hope not, my lady," said her mother. "'Tis a match which will double your father's power in Scotland, and your own wealth, one fine day." Her head, swathed in white linen and grey hodden, nodded knowingly.

"But, madam mother, I should prefer to stay here, working with my father ... or to enter an enclosed order ... than to marry a man I do not, nay, cannot love!"

"Scullery maid talk!" exclaimed Lady Margaret.

"But, in France, now, it is becoming the fashion for even nobles to marry ladies of their choice."

"Be quiet, girl. 'Tis bad enough that you are a woman grown ... rising twenty ... and not yet wed. At the court of Holyrood last spring, I was an object of mockery that I had a daughter past marrying age, who yet hung about my skirts like a babe." Lady Margaret flushed as she spoke.

"If marry I must," said Dervorgilla, with spirit, "then could it not be a new man, someone who belongs to the age of liberty and grace which we approach? Balliol has the reputation of a wild man and impious. He blasphemes, is quick with his sword, he drinks ... and wenches,"

The girl's fire was dying down. "He would not even like me, Mama."

"Liking's got nothing to do with wedding," said Lady Margaret, flatly. "Your marriage date is set for next June. You and I will be busy enough arranging your trousseau between now and then to rid you of these vulgar notions."

"Aye," Alan interposed, "let's hear no more of

this nonsense now, my lass. It is not becoming. Why, your sister Helena married deQuincy these two years past without one murmur and when Christian's turn comes I doubt she'll hang upon the air for sic a puny tale as love!"

Lord Alan was tired of the scene. "Now, begone, daughter, about your alms-giving; go bath your pet pug, but trouble me no more with your maidishness; I have matters of urgency to talk of with your mother."

Dervorgilla's green gown, two shades darker than her eyes, whispered across the rushes as she bent her knee first to her father and then to her mother.

That lady said, "Send the page with the torches. It grows dark. And tell my maid of the wardrobe to await me in my chamber. I'll come straight."

Dervorgilla walked slowly from her father's quarters along the narrow gallery where the wind was keen. She knew there was no hope of avoiding marriage now. Come spring, she must be the bride of the coarse living Baron de Balliol. She shuddered with repulsion. Once, she'd thought she might have accepted the life of the cloister; but her suggestion to her father had not been whole-hearted. For all her sympathy with the sick and poor, for all her love of the common people of her native land who, in trouble, came to the castle for help, she loved life too much to be entirely drawn to the closed-in life of a religious.

Pausing at an opening on the stairway wall, she gazed down towards the dark waters of Loch Ken. Even in winter, she loved it. She loved this old home of her father's house. Kenmure was where she'd been born and much as she loved to visit her father's other properties, she had not the same heart-love for them. The early evening air was sharp. Mist rose over the loch. Dervorgilla shivered and thought with pleasure of the comfort of a fire; she ran on down the stairs, pushing open the door of a small chamber where a girl sat by a peat fire, idly plucking the strings of a small harp.

Without being aware of it, Dervorgilla sighed as she drew up a bench that she might sit and warm her feet.

"Dear me, Dev," a high pitched voice drawled. "It is as if you carried all the cares of Christendom." The red-headed girl laughed, too sharply, before continuing ... "and you about to make the match of the year!"

Christian's eyes glinted greedily in the firelight "I should purr for pleasure if I were marrying John de Balliol. He is so handsome, a *real* man unlike my betrothed, de Fortibus who is plain and ... boring! You will be rich ... you will have gowns, and jewels; horses, houses, servants. You will meet the highest not only in Scotland, but in England and in France too. Who knows what you might not ..."

"Oh, be quiet Christian. You know I don't really care about such things. Well yes, I like pretty clothes and a comfortable bed, good food and wine, but you know there's more to life than our creature comforts."

"Don't be such a prig, sister. Wait till you're an old lady with gouty knees ... then you may try to earn your place in Heaven by noble deeds and pious platitudes!"

"You don't understand," Dervogilla replied patiently. "It's just that ..."

But her sentence was never finished. As she spoke, the loud thundering sound of men beating upon the oaken door of the castle came from below.

Christian stopped her idle tinkering with the strings of her clairsach and ran to the narrow window. Pulling aside the leather hanging, she leaned out.

"I can't see," she exclaimed. "But I hear horses and men speaking ... I think there are many. Who on earth can it be?" Impatiently she called for a page. "Who has come? Is it our brother Thomas?" her eyes shone with excitement.

"I do not know, Lady Christian."

Christian flung her riding crop, lying on the table with her gloves and a heavy cape, at the lad ... "Find out. Idiot!"

"It wouldn't be Thomas. He's in Northumberland? Or is he, Christian?" Dervorgilla rose and took her sister by the shoulders, "Do you expect Thomas? Have you some news of him? Has he been scheming ...?"

"Let me be, Dev. I know nothing of Tom's plans"

The page ran into the room. His eyes were wide, "They say it's Adam, he's caught some of the Bruce of Annandale's men raiding our deer. And there's a strange band with them but I cannot find out who yet."

"Pooh!" Christian pouted. "Deer stealing, I thought it was something interesting." She sat down again beside the fire, stirring a small, shaggy dog as she did so. The dog moved over to where Dervorgilla sat, her hands loose in her lap. She picked up the small creature and began to fondle it.

Christian began to play a quiet tune, singing in a small voice. There was silence broken only by the splutter of the resin torch set in its wall bracket.

After a moment Christian said, gently malicious, "Aren't you going to intercede with father for the poor men caught stealing?"

Dervorgilla started to reply when their mother bustled into the room.

"There, Dev," she said, importantly, "there's a fine to-do. Your husband intended has come. It seems he was on his way here when he came upon Adam struggling to put down a band of the Bruce hooligans who were at our deer. Adam was glad of his help and they dispersed the varlets. Now, come, put on your gown of red wool and your gold circlet. You, too, Christian. Make yourself presentable. I must see the cooks.

It is well past four o'clock and your father wishes to dine."

She was gone, a small, plump whirlwind. Christian at once jumped up.

"No doubt," she said, gleefully, "your Balliol will be attended by some Norman knight." She ran her hands through her long red hair ... "Yes, I'll put on my new gown. You, I suppose, would rather sup in the hall with the beggars!"

"Christian, please" Dervorgilla said, as she set down the dog and moved towards the door. Her heart was heavy, but she knew that she must obey her parents' wishes. She moved towards her own chamber, calling for her tiring maid. She had only met Sir John once, briefly, at a tourney at Barnard Castle, his estate in Durham, two years earlier. She remembered him as a barrel of a man, strong as a war horse, with thick, red lips, a heavy accent, and his hair was dark with slight greying ... He was old! Not so old as her father but far too old to be her husband, Dervorgilla thought.

The long dining hall was hot. And noisy. Two boys stood beside the cavernous fireplace, piling on peats and wood continuously. The sconces spluttered, adding their spicy scent to the peat reek. There was a crowd of warriors and their men about the lower table; dogs scuffled among the rushes, eager for the tit-bits which they hoped would come their way.

There was a stir of servants; a clash of platters, shouting from the men and maids serving their betters; from the kitchen passageway a reek of food wafted.

At the high table, there was scarcely more order. Lord Alan and his family sat facing down the long hall, the women ranged to his right. Next to him, on his left, sat the guest of honour, Baron de Balliol. Beside him sat Balliol's knight, and in varying degrees of precedence sat the lesser household dignitaries. These included Adam, Lord Alan's most trusted steward, the family priest and the Lady Eleanor, widow of Adam's predecessor; who had taken charge of the younger children in the household, and now acted as a companion to them.

Dervorgilla sat next to her sister who was seated beside their mother. She could not see her middle-aged suitor and was glad of it. Behind her chair, stood Kate, her personal maid and dearest friend.

On her left, Christian still continued to torment her throughout the meal.

With her horn mug of watered wine in her hand, the younger sister leaned towards Dev.

"If you will not have Balliol, I will. He is a real man," she whispered. "He would know how to pleasure his wife!"

"For shame, Chris, be quiet. Mother will hear you!"

"I don't care. I long to be wed. It's what a woman is meant for. Besides, I'm tired of being ordered around by mother and old Madam Eleanor. I want to be mistress of my own castle, to order the servants, to buy new gowns, to eat what I like, when I like."

Dervorgilla continued eating the roast fowl on the wooden trencher before her. She watched the glimmering light play upon her finely chased silver knife and two-pronged fork.

"All those things I want, too," she replied. "And even a man. I'm not such a milksop fool as you think, I should love to have babies. But not with a man who is old and lecherous."

"Who cares? If he's old, then he'll die all the sooner and you will be a rich widow. Oh, that t'were I," the younger girl pouted. She leaned forward a little to gaze along the table. She wanted to catch Balliol's eye. All she could see was a corner of his square cut, grey-flecked beard, his heavy hands cutting his fowl, fast, lifting his goblet often. She heard him roar with laughter at something her father said. There was a full bodied quality to his voice which thrilled Christian. Damn Dervorgilla being the one to get him! She and this virile knight from Normandy could have matched each other like eagles. An idea began to torment her. Perhaps Thomas would help her? If she promised him money? For, if wife she could not be, the marriage papers *were* already sealed after all, it was true there were other things a woman might be in a man's life. Sometimes their influence was greater than that of a legal wife. Look at Edith Swan-Neck, all those hundreds of years ago she'd been but Harold, the Saxon's, hand-fast wife, and anyone knew what that meant. And what of the illicit passion of Guenevere and Lancelot and those other ancient knights that the minstrels sang of?

Dervorgilla with her ideals of "love" might pine and shrink from a true man; but there were other ways of a man and a maid just as important as this flimsy "love". Who needed such high-flown whimsies? There were elemental bonds, vital, not to be denied. These were what mattered, thought Christian, wiping her hands on her fine white napkin with the embroidered initial, her brown eyes glowing. Balliol might have to be Dev's, legally, but he could be hers in the way that mattered; and if she bore him a son, even out of wedlock, *that* would hold him!

There was a scraping of chairs on the stone floor. Deep in her thoughts, Christian had not noticed that her father's chaplain had spoken his grace and that Lord Alan and his lady were leading their guest and his squire to the small, private solar above stairs. Lady Margaret signed to her two daughters to follow.

In the small chamber it was draughty, after the heat of the crowded hall. The new green glass window was ill fitting and the draped skin covering it moved like a restless animal as the winter wind sought its unlawful entries. The Lady Margaret sent her page for a fur pelisse.

Sir John walked towards Dervorgilla as she came into the room,

"So, my bride," he boomed, taking her hand

in his bigger one. "The seals are upon the papers. In the summer of the new year, we shall be wed. Where shall it be?"

Dervorgilla coloured, lowered her eyelids to hide her panicking eyes. After a moment's uncomfortable pause, "At Dundrennan, please my lord," she said in a small voice. "I love it dearly."

"Very well, madam. And afterwards we will travel to Picardy, There will be affairs to attend to at Bailleul-en-Vimeu. It is pleasant there in June."

"And afterwards may we return and stay a while at Botel, my father's small castle upon the Urr? It is to be part of my dower and I love it best of all there, and in the heart of summer it is the loveliest place on earth."

"Certainly, if you wish it." Sir John smiled slightly and Dervorgilla felt she had been naive. She flushed and was glad when her father moved towards them. Why must she marry this worldly baron? This was called the age of liberty; yet she was not free to dispose of her life as she would. Rebellion made Dervorgilla's green eyes sparkle suddenly, so that her betrothed, looking at her in the firelight, thought momentarily that perhaps she was less of a milk and water maid than he'd first thought. But his mind was more interested in what his future father-in-law was saying.

"Thomas? Nay, I heard nothing of him in Yorkshire. Say you so? With the Bruces?"

"Robert the Bruce of Annandale, though he

be kith to me ... our common great-grandfather was King David, God rest him ... has long coveted my lands."

Lord Alan continued "Young though he is, Thomas my son, being what he is, born outside the law, and a lameter into the bargain, cannot forgive me for it. He covets what my daughters must lawfully inherit some day soon. I fear he is intriguing with Annandale."

"Certainly they were Annandale's men who were raiding your forest this day. But I saw none of Thomas the Bastard's men, I would know some of them; they raided my lands in Durham last year. Right soundly did we trounce them." The strong white teeth gleamed with glee. "I marked two of them myself. I doubt not but I could recognise them. Yet I saw none of them in this last affray."

"Look you for them, though, in all that stands against the House of Alan. The Bruces, I know well, mean trouble for us. Which is why I welcome right heartily this match between our two houses. Your power, allied to Dervogilla's, will secure the crown of Galloway for many a generation to come, God willing."

"Tell me," Balliol leaned towards the elder man, "People speak of you as 'King Alan'. But 'tis not so, in law?"

"Nay, not in law, it's true. But Galloway is a land unto itself as you know. We call it a Kingdom. The good God made us to stand apart from the main body of Scotland as Galwegians.

My wife has the royal blood, her uncles Malcolm the Maid and William the Lion both being Kings of Scotland. And since my grandfather, Fergus, held the overlordship of Galloway, we are used to say we have royal authority, at least for our being called 'Kings' of Galloway. The common people, you know, believe us so to be."

"Well, a name's but a name," Balliol turned away to warm himself by the glowing peats. As he did so, he was startled to see the younger of his host's two girls looking at him in a way which could not be mistaken, Hussy! the baron thought. But, as his eye took in the lines of her supple figure, an interesting enough hussy, perhaps. No doubt the knightly past-time of chivalry was played here as well as by the gallants and ladies of the south, and of the Norman lands. True, this cold, wild land seemed over-full of saints and priests. Yet, surely good red blood coursed through the veins of the people. But, thought Balliol, to idle with one's wife's sister would be dangerous. Far too dangerous!

Realising that Balliol had noticed her, Christian boldly approached him. "Sir John," she began, then, pertly smirking "brother John, mayn't I say? Tell us about Magna Carta. You were there as a signatory, I know. Our father never tells us what passed there and I have always wondered. Was not the king sore vexed at being forced to sign such a charter?"

Sir John threw back his magnificent black head and roared, that same bull's roar of male gustiness which had earlier stirred Christian.

"Marry," he spluttered. "'Tis not only a blithesome wench, but one who would speak of State matters into the bargain."

Lord Alan turned scowling at Christian. When would this pert daughter of his learn to behave? The Lady Margaret, conscious that her daughter's boldness reflected poorly upon her own motherly training, took Christian's hand in hers, and beckoned to Dervorgilla.

"Before we go to bed," she intervened, "there are three sick among our servants who need attention and the friar is waiting to speak to me about the service tomorrow. You will excuse us, Sir John. We shall see you tomorrow."

"Goodnight, ladies," said Balliol. He found it unnecessary to disguise his lack of regret that the women were retiring. He had matters of more interest to discuss with Lord Alan. Women had a part to play in a man's life, but it was not an important one.

Christian could not sleep. Her mother's scolding tongue did not worry her. She was used to it. But although she could hear the late owls hooting beyond her chamber wall, her thoughts were in a turmoil, her heart beat wildly. Desire surged through her. She had seen the Norman baron's appraisal of her. It was dangerous, for if they were discovered, it could mean war between the two houses. A man should not play fast and loose so close to home. The Church would call it a mortal sin; for Christian the thought of the possible danger to her soul merely added a spice of interest. In spite of old cat Eleanor's watchful eye, and her mother's frank warnings about taming the heat of her blood ... Christian was not entirely inexperienced in matters of the flesh. There were one or two of the young squires sent to learn their trade at her father's court, who had helped her to explore love's by-ways.

She would! She would risk excommunication, hellfire even, she shivered, but then, after all, the winter air was chill ... she must. The fire in her blood could only be quenched by one thing.

Quietly, she slipped on her soft doe-skin shoes, wrapped a fur pelisse around her. The rush taper burned fitfully. Fortunately, her maid, Nance, was one of those suffering from the winter fever, so she was unusually alone in her chamber. She thanked God that, being past seventeen, she no longer slept in the long upper chamber with all the other green girls. Where had they lodged Sir John? Feverishly, she tried to remember what she had heard her mother telling the castellan. Yes! That was it. In the lakeside turret, to the north. It was not far, if she took the small winding stair used by the page-boys when they brought up the washing water.

In the stone corridors the torches were burning low. But Christian knew her way and felt the shadows to be her friends. Soon, she had reached the oaken door behind which Sir John slept. She saw that Sir John had no page sleeping at his threshold. Why no servant on guard?

Could it be that he had expected her visit? Urgently she scratched at the door. There was no answer. Feverishly she scratched again; to knock too loudly was to court investigation but having got so far Christian was determined to get her way. She shook the string of the latch. It sounded horribly loud. Oh, it was so cold. Here the windows were neither glazed nor curtained. A particularly strong gust of wind almost doused the sconce at the end of the passage.

The door opened. The torch flared up and showed the man who held the door ajar, the red hair and eager lips of the girl standing in the passage, her fur pelisse showing the gleam of white limbs. God's Breath! But she was bold indeed. A willing wench in truth. For a long moment the two gazed at each other. Balliol was a sensual man and the sight of the beauty before him stirred his senses all too quickly. He reached out a hand towards her.

Then his sense of the fitness of things, something akin to the warning sense of danger which alerts animals to moments of peril, grew stronger.

"Go back to your sleep girl. You know this cannot be. There is too much at stake. If I take you ... and I could, you would be worthy of the having, I don't doubt ... it could mean war between your father and myself. Excommunication even ..."

"you speak like my sister!" spat out Christian.

"... or worse, death" continued Balliol

implaccably. "Go back now before we are discovered."

"But you told me ... with your eyes ... YOU told me," Christian breathed, frantically, "you wanted me."

"Don't be a fool, girl. I want many women. All men do. But for a few minutes' pleasure of the flesh, would I risk so much? If you must play the harlot, play it with someone who has less at stake. Christ's bones, sister-in-law go ... GO, now, before we are discovered and your father's men come upon us."

Balliol pushed Christian towards the end of the corridor, towards the staircase. Unbelieving, half weeping with frustration and humiliation, she went.

Chapter Two

The piteous yowling filled the bedchamber and awoke Dervorgilla. Was it a wolf? Could not be ... they were all away to their summer lairs atop Bengairn and Screel. There it was again, loud, insistent. Oh mercy, it was her kittling, Mousie, so called because of her phenomenal skill in catching the mice which infested the castle even though she was little more than a kitten. Dervorgilla jumped out of her bed, naked as she always was at night, opened the new-fangled window, with its green bottle glass which certainly did hold back the cold night air; yes, it was Mousie, clinging perilously to the ivy which covered the granite wall and clearly terrified. Shivering in the cobweb of thin drizzle she reached for the cat and brought her into the warmth of the bed where the creature purred and rolled with relief and pleasure at her rescue from peril.

"Oh, Mousie, my wee pet ... it is scarce light yet; I shall not get back to my dreams and now I must endure the ill thoughts that go round and round in my head." She cuddled the ginger cat to her, thinking, "This night I shall not lie in my father's castle of Kenmure; I shall not gaze down on long, silvery, treacherous Loch Ken. Tonight I shall lie at the Castle of Wraiths and look over to Kinderloch ..." she caught her breath "and I shall not lie alone! This time tomorrow I shall be the wife of Baron Balliol." She bit her lip in apprehension as there came the quiet knocking at her bedroom door. The young apprentice serving-maid who slept on the bench at the foot of her bed was yet snoring, awoke and slowly went, yawning like a gaping gosling, to open the door.

"Oh, 'tis you, Kate ... is't waking hour?" The lassie turned to her mistress; sketching a curtsey she said,"Lady Dervorgilla, Kate be here."

"Aye, I'm here right enough." She moved to the bed ... 'tis time to rise, my lady ..." then she gave a small yell. "For our Lord's sake, whit hev ye there ... well, if it's no' that kitlin' ye dote on! How came she in your bed?"

Dervorgilla sat up against her linen pillow and laughed quietly. "She came through ivy and by yon new-fangled glass window's crack."

Her mood changed swiftly. "Oh, Kate ... have you seen the day? It is weeping, as I would weep; I cannot bear the thought of leaving my home and my family to go away with this ... this ... stranger knight. I don't want to be a wife ..." the tears began to flow.

"Fie, my bonny dearie. Dry your water spouts, rise, take your bath and let me dress you in your wedding claes ... you'll be a bonnie lass for sure

in your scarlet gown and your gold leather shoon ... forbye your golden head band and your pearls and rubies from your grandfather King David."
Kate, Dervorgilla's personal maid and lifelong confidante would stand no maidish pettedness.

"But, even the day weeps for me, June though it be." Dervorgilla replied.

"Good my lady, slip into this bath 'ere the water cools ... and, I have strewn the tub with rosemary, with Lad's Love, e'en with a pickle o' the very first lavender." Reluctantly, Dervorgilla did as she was bid.

Soon she was dry and putting on her cambric nether garments, her boned bodice, and her cambric and her silken petticoats. Still she looked downcast, still she sighed as she watched the morning haar hang at her window.

Kate shook her head. "My lassie," she said, kindly as she brought the scarlet wedding robe of best Lyons brocade to her mistress. "Sit ye doon on the dressing stool ... take up yon siller looking glass, pinch your cheeks till the colour comes in and I will dress your hair. We maun be ready, before long," glancing out of the now-opened window, "I wager this morning mist will blow away and by the time you reach the Abbey of Dundrennan, the sun will shine on ye."

"Dundrennan," Dervorgilla repeated slowly ... "it's nearly one hundred years since my grandfather King David founded that serene sanctuary ... I'm glad the marriage is to take place there ... I've always found peace ..."

"Dervorgilla, are you nearly clad?" Lady Margaret bustled excitedly into the room. "the servants are bringing you a morning breakfast ... eat something of it, do. At ten of the clock your father will come to fetch you ... oh", her hand flew to her flushed cheek ... "I forgot to tell you ... yet another wedding present has come ... from the Annandale Bruces ... your cousins at Lochmaben ... and what do you think it is?"

"I don't know," Dervorgilla replied. She didn't much care for that branch of the family and, like her father, Alan, suspected they might one day stir up trouble when it came ... if it came ... to a dispute about the heir to the Scots throne.

Scarcely drawing breath, Lady Margaret rushed on eagerly. "Why, they have sent the noblest pair of soar-hawks you ever saw and a pure white merlin for your use in hunting! Caparisoned richly too, with harness of finest Spanish tooled leather."

At this news Dervorgilla's spirits rose a little. She loved to ride out, whether it be a gentle canter along Loch Ken side or, in the autumn, to follow the sport of chasing the hare or the roe deer over her father's land.

Lady Margaret's excitement abated a little.

"Dervorgilla," she said gently. "All will be well. Your bridegroom is a good man and you will be a good wife. The match is a prudent one for both of our families ... with our combined lands and wealth ..." she raised her eyebrows in a meaningful expression, almost licking her lips in appreciation of their good fortune as Dervorgilla interrupted with her oft-repeated caveat ... "but only if I loved him ... or he might ever love me."

"Child, love may well grow. Your father and I did not 'marry for love' as you continually sigh, but our marriage, our family, have brought us as close as anyone might want. Now, put on your family jewels then rest a little; the ceremony will be brief enough but the wedding feast will take all your strength ere you rest at Wraiths tonight." The small figure richly dressed herself, flew out of the room.

Dervorgilla sighed and began to stroke her beloved kitten, now curled in sleep upon her counterpane.

"Ma doo," Kate said, "dinnae sigh ... your mother speaks truly ... all will be well ... and see ..." she gestured to the window ... "as I telt ee, thon lowerin' haar is lifting and ye ken, 'Happy the bride the sun shines on.'"

At ten o'clock, Lord Alan of Galloway arrived and escorted his beautiful daughter to the great hall where her six bridesmaids awaited. They were lovely in their pale gold silken gowns, chaplets of ivory roses in their hair, tussie-mussies of fresh garden flowers in their hands. They all smiled and curtseyed to the bride.

Dervorgilla remembered nothing of the slow-paced ride in the four-horse litter which took her through the lanes festooned with wild roses and early honeysuckle. But for the rest of her life she remembered the solemn and moving service in the grey stone Abbey of Dundrennan, remembered, too, the clear song of a sole blackbird in the pause just before she uttered the words "I will" which bound her forever to the imposing man at her side whom she scarcely knew.

Soon they were back at Kenmure Castle, The banquet was lavish as befitted a king's grand-daughter; the wines were from her new husband's French estates; it was both superb in quality and endless in quantity. The two hundred or more guests were carousing merrily when through the din of laughter, of dogs growling at each other's scraps, of servants scurrying with platters of roast boar, whole pigeons and every roast or broiled fish or fowl one could wish for came a sudden angry sound of raised voices at the top table where the immediate bridal party sat.

A youth, somewhat lame, hair tousled, colour flaming and clearly affected by having drunk too much wine, was unsteadily listing to the right and to left as he accosted Lord Alan at the high table. It was Thomas the Bastard, half brother to Dervorgilla, from an unchancy liasion of her father's youth.

"And why I am not in my rightful place with the close family? I may have been born on the wrong side of the blankets yet am I your son, Sir." The spittle frothed at the corners of his mouth. The young man's speech was rough, the words ill-formed.

Anxiously, Dervorgilla spoke to her bridegroom, as the fellow's hand moved to the dagger at his waist.

"'tis Thomas, my half-brother; he is a lameter and a malcontent ... mayhap with some reason. He is not quite in full possession of his wits," ... she began to rise from her seat ... "but I could always calm him."

"My lady," Balliol said, putting a restraining hand on her arm, "it is not fitting that you should leave your place to deal with this madman. I will go."

"No, Sir John, in his fear of your strength and power he could attempt some rashnesss to you, and himself, some dreadful harm. He will listen to me, all our days I have been the one to calm his rages. I beg you," and she gave him a little bob of a curtsey, as if to placate her new husband, "give me leave to go to him."

Dervorgilla slipped quietly from her place, reached her swaying half brother and put protective arms about him. She glanced towards their father, now on his feet, his face purple with supressed rage and began to steer the drunken boy from the room. Two of her father's squires took the now almost collapsed drunkard into their care. Dervorgilla slipped back to retake her seat beside her new husband. He raised his horn goblet of fine French wine to her and kissed her hand, his eyes glinting with admiration.

"God's wounds, madam," he said softly. "'twas bravely done." Dervorgilla blushed scarlet. "He will sleep and by morning have forgotten this blunder" ... she smiled her sweet, understanding smile.

"Madam," her husband replied. "The hour grows late. I believe we should quit this revelry and make our way to Wraiths."

"As you wish, Sir John" Dervorgilla replied.

Three hours travel later, Dervorgilla in her comfortable litter drawn by four horses, her husband riding his own brown mare slightly ahead of her, with their retinue behind them, reached the small castle of Wraiths, overlooking the Solway Firth, with the bulk of Criffel Hill behind them.

Dervorgilla went straight to the bedchamber which was to be hers and Balliol's; Kate was waiting for her, as she took Dervorgilla's light wool cape from her and began to unlace her shoes they could hear Balliol ordering his squires and servants. With Kate's help, Dervorgilla took off her elaborate jewels, removed the golden gown and filet and shook out her long hair. Soon she wore her wedding night robe of palest turquoise linen. "Thank you, Kate" she said. "I confess I am considerably weary."

"Yes, my lady, it has been a long day." replied Kate.

A masculine voice, deep and low came from the doorway,

"It has been a long day, in sooth." Balliol

nodded kindly to Kate. "You may go now girl; and in the morning do not awaken your mistress early, let her lie."

Kate curtseyed and left.

Dervorgilla's heart began to race.

Balliol approached Dervorgilla who stood beside the small log fire.

"My dear lady," he said, speaking gently, tenderly. "It has been a long day ... for us all." He smiled, suddenly looking younger, almost boyish. "Even I am tired as I know you are." Dervorgilla smiled in return, somewhat nervously. Her heart was still pounding.

"We are to be man and wife for many a year ahead, God willing. There is no necessity to complete the ceremony of our union this morning by a physical union. Time enough for that, I vow." The big man bowed before his new wife; he took each of her hands in his own and kissed them softly. "Goodnight my Dervorgilla" he said, kissing her cheeks. "We shall meet tomorrow ... let us say " he smiled again ... "at noon. Sleep well, my wife."

Chapter Three

In the circle of the low hills, within sound of the gentle river Urr gliding its way to the firth, where it would join the dream-blue waters of the Solway, Dervorgilla sat, under the shade of a fir tree. In her lap lay the gurgling baby Cecily, whose eyes were as blue as the summer sky above them.

Here, in the garden at Botel, with its stone walks interspersed with sweet, clove-smelling gilly-flowers, with poppies and mignonette, Balliol's wife was supremely happy. Kate sat beside them, sewing quietly. A little brown terrier was pretending to chase rats around the trunks of the trees. There was a sound of bees in the air and the scent of the honeysuckle climbing along the grey stone dyke was very sweet.

"Here, Tam," Dervorgilla called, softly, not to alarm the baby. "If he goes too far, he'll get lost, and dear knows when we'd ever see him again. Fetch him, Kate, there's a good lass."

"You and yon pup," grumbled Kitty. "He's mair to you than yer ain bairn." She smiled to soften the remark. There was no impudence in it for Kitty, but two years the younger, had grown up with Dervorgilla, as her personal playmate, first, then as her own body-servant. They had no secrets between them and, indeed, Dervorgilla often thought she wished Kitty had been her own sister for she was far more to her liking than the waspish, wanton Christian, or than Helena whom she rarely saw since now she lived most of the time in the south of England.

Kitty brought the rough-haired little terrier to his mistress and set him down beside her outspread green silk skirt.

"There, you wee besom, you. See and be still!" She gave him a light daud on the ear. Tammy grinned at her and licked Dervorgilla's hand as it came out to fondle his sandy fur.

"He's been a good friend to me these last two years," she said, smiling.

"Ye've had better than a dog for company," Kitty insinuated, nodding knowingly over her mending. She jerked her round chin at Cecily, crowing contentedly in her mother's lap "And there's the proof of it!"

"You're growing bawdy, Kate. It ill becomes you," Dervorgilla returned, her colour deepening. But she was not ill pleased.

"Ye've gotten yersel' a right man, I've nae doubt. You that was so feared to enter the marriage bed."

Dervorgilla's green eyes deepened and her face bloomed with sudden emotion.

"He is a man, Kit, that I'll agree. And far less ill to deal with than I'd ever dreamt."

"Aye. He may bark and even bite at some of us, but I've never heard a bad word from him to you. Nor should he need to bark at you for if you've gotten a guid man, I'm mortal shair he'd never find a more docile lass to wife him."

"I'm not so docile," Dervorgilla threw back her head and laughed with rich enjoyment.

"But," she continued, loving to discuss this husband of hers whom she found, after thirteen months of marriage, daily more fascinating, "my lord Balliol is a great man; I love it when he talks to me as he does sometimes … of affairs of state. He reminds me a little of my grand-father."

"He's far mair a lion than yon saintly lamb," Kitty interpolated sturdily.

"I know. They are not at all alike really, save in their command of men and affairs. But, there is a … a … largeness of mind which I like. My lord is never unjust, although he may be hasty …"

"He's no' ower pious, either," Kitty put in, biting off her thread.

"No. That is something which troubles me; he is impatient of the church and he believes her bishops should be less powerful. Yet he is not an unbeliever, Kate." Dervorgilla looked suddenly anxious.

"Ah weel, many of us may be that and yet none the waur o't," said Kitty plainly, standing up to brush the threads from her brown linen skirt.

"And how's ma wee pettie?" she clucked, bending over small Cecily. "My but she's bonny.

A real love-child … a child of love," she corrected herself, giggling.

"Not really," Dervorgilla took up the thought seriously. "But … mayhap the next babe will be, for," in a sudden rush of confidence, "truth to tell, Kate, I could find it in me, now, to love Sir John with all my heart and soul, only …" she looked sad. "I do not think he wants love from me. I believe he is not …" she paused, unwilling to put the thought into words.

"No always wi' time for domestic joys"? Kate nodded wisely. "Ah well, he's a busy man at the height of his powers. What else could ye expec' and him aye travellin' from one bit to anither."

"Kitty," Dervorgilla said, straightening her back and shifting her cramped legs, "I sometimes wish we were not SO wealthy. There is rarely time for us to speak to each other save on business concerning some property … either his, or mine. I envy the simple folk."

"Aye," Kit interrupted "The mair ye own the mair ye groan. That's what my auld faither used to say. Dear knows, as a plain gaird'ner, he never owned nocht worth the counting."

"But it's true", Dervorgila said "I'm sure riches …"

"What's true?" said a man's deep voice. Half-turning towards the grey castle walls, Dervorgilla saw her father coming towards her, leaning on Christian's arm.

"What's true, my dear?" he asked.

"Oh … that property, wealth, brings too

many cares. Leaves us no time for ourselves."

"Aye. It's so. It brings many responsibilities. We have much to do. Fighting our enemies," he sighed, "to protect what is ours; staving off the demands of our betters, too." Lord Alan looked tired. Dervorgilla noticed how grey his skin was.

He brightened as he spoke again. "But my grandfather once told me something which has given me much heart. 'Remember,' he said, 'we nobles hold the key to the future. It is to us that the common people look for all their learning, their well-being, their advancement. We are not only leaders of fighting men, holders of land. Through us must come the learning and the advancement of the ages.' It's a thought to cherish when care presses too hard."

Christian sat down beside Dervorgilla and put out a finger to the baby who was waving her small hands in the air,

"You are all too high-flown," she pouted. "The serfs don't want to learn. They are happy in their dirty hovels, so long as we give them enough to eat and something to keep the worst of the cold at bay. When Albermarle and I are wed, I shall leave the dispensation of alms to my steward. I intend to enjoy my life at the English court. Thanks to my father's skills in managing my dowry and the marriage settlement, I shall be rich, at last. I shall own gowns of finest silk, jewels from Italy; we shall drink wine every day ... good wine! And I shall do nothing but play with my babies, write songs for my minstrels to sing ... and a few other things!" Her sharp features were, for once, soft, as she gave her finger to the baby's tiny grasp.

"Yes," thought Dervorgilla, "I know what 'other things' mean. Affairs of the heart. Gallantry is one thing, but Chris goes too far. She's lucky not to have been caught before this, either by mother or Lady Eleanor. Well, as a married woman, she'll certainly have more freedom; and London's court is licentious enough to allow for anything."

"Isn't she a bonny wee pet?" Kitty asked Christian.

"She's adorable," Christian said, "May I hold her, Dev?"

She lifted the baby with a kind of fierce eagerness, cradling her to her breast and crooning to her.

Strange, thought Dev, how Christian adores babies. So unlike her. But then, people are never "like"; we are all full of the oddest contradictions.

"Dervorgilla," the old man broke into her thoughts. "I had a message from your husband this morning. This is why we rode over from Kenmure. It seems there is some trouble on your Isle of Man property." Dervorgilla looked attentively at her father.

"The Vikings are not attacking again?"

"No. Nothing so drastic, or I'd need to call my navy into action. No. It's a dispute about the fishing rights off the shore of that portion of your dower which I granted you from my first wife's lands, d'you remember, at Alington?"

"I cannot think where you mean, father. I know that land is now mine, but you never took me to Man and it means little, I confess."

Alan sighed and stirred on the bench uneasily. He put his hand to his side.

"What is it, father? Are you not well?"

"This old pain. It comes back. But I'm all right. Wench," he said, turning to Kitty standing a respectful distance off, playing with Tammy. "Fetch me a posset. Tell your cook to make it hot and to keep the wine low but to add leaves of peppermint. It relieves me," he added, turning again to his daughters.

"I could go myself, to deal with this affair. But ... I fear I'm tired; I have asked Sir John to go. And in his letter to me today he writes that he will go forthwith and that he would like you to go with him."

"Go to Man? I'd love to." Dervorgilla was stirred and proud to think that her husband wanted her to go with him. It was the first time he had suggested that she travel with him since their honeymoon in Normandy. True, she had been pregnant shortly afterwards and not fit to travel until lately. But on his recent visits to Durham to deal with some boundary dispute on his land there, and on his visit to Henry's court in London he had bid her stay at Botel.

"When does he want me to go?"

"In two weeks time. He will come himself by

Saturday and you can make your plans."

"You'll be away for my wedding," pouted Christian, looking up from playing with Cecily, who crowed excitedly at her aunt's attentions.

"Shall we, father? will it take so long."

"Mayhap. The Abbot of Ramsey's a powerful enough man and will dispute right stoutly for his church's gain."

"His own," put in Christian. "I know these abbots; greedy men, who grow fat doing nothing. Make sure you fight hard, Dev."

"Sir John will do that, I'm sure." Lord Alan said. "And I'm thankful that he can and will, for I grow old and can no longer do all as I did formerly."

"Father, have you seen the physician?"

"Yes, daughter. He can do little but bleed me from time to time. And your mother cossets me ... almost too well," he added, wryly.

"Here's your draught, sir," Kitty came with a horn mug, covered and wrapped in a linen napkin. "It's warm yet."

"So, Dev ... you will miss my wedding. 'Tis vexing for it's to be a great affair you know. My gown is sumptuous. The king's likely to attend, and half the nobles of Scotland." Vanity shone in Christian's eyes. "Fortibus is a wealthy man and likes a wife to display his riches!"

Yes, thought Dervorgilla sadly, it is not for your new husband's rheumy eyes you will parade your attractions. Other men, younger, more virile, were what Chris sought.

"If we can be back from Man, we will be there," she promised her younger sister now, smiling gently at her. How much softer Chris looked as she nursed Cecily! If only she could show more of her better self! "Faugh!" Christian exclaimed, holding the bundle of white, soft linen out ... "Kitty ... Kitty ... take her; she's wet me! Faugh! How disgusting. I must wash ... oh, ... even my gown is marked ..." she jumped up, her mood of gentleness vanished.

Her father laughed. "Babes have a way of damping their elders, lassie." he chuckled.

"But they should not damp our fastidious, fine lady," came a new, sardonic voice.

The young man limping down the flag-stones was unhealthily thin, shorter than either Christian or Dervorgilla, and his pock-marked face was adorned with a gingery fringe of whiskers.

"Tom!" cried Christian. "What are you doing here?"

Kitty, the damp baby held securely to her bosom, ducked a hasty curtsey to Lord Alan, and moved past the newcomer, towards the castle.

Tammy, left to his own devices, ran towards the young man, sniffing at his ankles. Tom kicked clumsily at the terrier, who ran off to resume his rat hunting.

"Sir," Tom ducked his head in a cursory greeting to his father. "Chris, Dev." He made a mock bow to the young women.

"Hallo, Tom," Dervorgilla replied. This half-brother of hers made her uncomfortable always. His small eyes seemed to look lasciviously through her gown. She knew he hated and envied his three half-sisters for being legitimate and the indisputable heirs to their fathers' estates. She knew too, how he had, for the past five years at least - indeed almost since he was scarcely old enough to understand such matters, even, intrigued with their cousin Bruce of Annandale. She feared him. There was an aura of evil about him. He meant to bring trouble to the House of Alan, she was sure. Yet, looking at his drawn, unhappy face and crippled right leg, she felt pity, too. He had much to bear. God was not always kind, it seemed.

"What brings you here?" his father asked.

"I want to speak to you. I was riding from Dumfries to Kirkcudbright, where I go to see some nags brought from Ireland. And on the way, I began to think ..." he paused, his little eyes shifting from one to another of the small group.

"Not now," Dervorgilla stretched out a hand to him, placing it on his tunic sleeve. "Our father is not well. Could you not wait ... some other day?"

"No. It must be today." Thomas's mouth set in a hard line.

Christian remained silent. She thought she knew what Thomas wanted and only hoped he would not give away to their father her own part in that scheme.

"Let him speak," Lord Alan said wearily.

"Since ever I can remember, you have spurned me," Thomas said, bitterly.

"Nay, lad. It is not so. You have thought so, and made yourself miserable in the thinking. But it is not so."

Thomas was growing angry. "It is," he muttered; then he burst out,

"Father, I am a man grown now. I am twenty, yet I go like a pauper. Barely enough money to support a band of followers; bastard I may be and nothing to be done about it I suppose; yet am I a noble's bastard ... a King's, the men of Galloway would say. And as such, I should be fittingly endowed."

"My son," said Alan, patiently, holding his side again, as if in fresh pain, and carefully setting down his mug upon the stone seat beside him, "many a Lord's younger son ... and that you are, in standing, I grant ... must seek his fortune by taking arms for some other noble. I have offered to give you destriers, armour and a suitable following of men to join some other Christian knight in Italy, or Spain; or to go to the Crusades in the Holy Land, e'en you will. I cannot give you a fortune. I am a rich man, I acknowledge it thankfully. But my riches are in my land, here in Galloway, in your mother's estates in Northampton and Hertford. Silver in the strongbox there is I grant you but not so much that I can hand you a fortune to squander. Besides, can you not wait till I die?" Lord Alan gave a grimace and moved to an easier position. "Mayhap it will not be so long. Your portion of my lands will come to you then. I have made some provision for you, lad." He smiled, albeit wanly, at the angry fellow before him.

"Some provision! Yes ... that's it. Some! And these maids will inherit all your vast wealth. I am the son. Your only son! I demand that you treat me as such. To be born on the wrong side of the blanket is nothing. Half the great men of England and Scotland were so born. Yet they have lands, wealth, armies ... I will not be flouted ... passed over like some ..."

Dervorgilla moved closer to her half-brother. "Thomas," she said, shaking him a little, "can you not see our father's unwell? I beg you leave him. My husband will be here by the week's end. Could you not talk to us then? Perhaps we could help you ... find some way to ..."

"Balliol?" spluttered Thomas. "That bold baron! Why, he is too proud even to acknowledge muck like me ... .but I've got something for him that he will not ..." Here, prudence overcame anger and Thomas held his tongue for a moment before bursting out.

"If you will not give me what is mine by right as your only male heir, I will take steps ..."

Here Dervorgilla placed her pale hand across the spluttering lips of the young man. Stately, with a sudden authority, she over-topped him by four inches.

"Be quiet!" she commanded. She felt a quiet strength in her.

For a moment or two, he was quiet, shocked into speechlessness by the strength and dignity his half-sister had so unexpectedly shown.

"Come, father," Dervorgilla said, raising the old man. "The sun's going down and you will be chilled. Come indoors. You must stay with me tonight here. I will send a messenger to Kenmure that Mother may know you are in my care."

Unprotesting, Lord Alan allowed himself to be led towards the path.

"Christian," Dervorgilla said, turning her head back towards the pair who stood in the deepening light, "come too, and bring Thomas. Do not be so wrathful, brother. Come, drink a cup in good fellowship ere you go on your way to Kirkcudbright."

Christian nodded, vaguely. Thomas merely glared at the departing figures.

As soon as their father and sister were out of earshot, Christian hissed at her half-brother,

"You are an oaf. A dolt. You will lose all if you cannot rein in your impatience."

"Keep your viper's tongue still" he retorted. "You do not know how I am pressed."

"More gambling debts? And fancy women?"

"What of it?" he flashed, "I'm a man, like other men even though I may be cursed by my birth."

"Christian ..." his mood changed. He had lost

his bitterness. Now he was pleading, "Christian ... you swear you will help me once you are married? Does de Fortibus know of your plans? Can you be sure of getting the money?"

"Tuts, little man. So many anxieties." Christian tossed her coppery curls. "I have told you, I can twist that old fop Fortibus round my little finger. He is mad for me." She laughed, with a brittle note in her voice. "Well ... he shall have me. But at a price. Money and freedom to do as I will." She laughed again. "Oh yes, brother dear. You can be sure of me." Suddenly serious. "But can I be sure of you? Will you keep your part of the bargain?"

"To help you win Balliol's attentions? By God's breath, Chris, I cannot see why you should want to run such a risk ... You will be burnt for incest."

"There is no blood tie," she said, sulkily.

"Holy Church says the tie is too close. Pick youself some other man. Balliol is a high-nosed worldling. Even if he wanted you, which he doesn't. He plays the game secretly, taking some serving wench quietly, when it suits him; but in public, always the perfect married man, correct, above reproach."

"You are wrong, Thomas. Balliol hates the church and will not accept her authority. He bows the knee to no man; even the King of England consults him ... or his purse, rather ... He's a passionate man, I swear, even though he plays the great lord. Anyway whatever he is, I want him!" Christian shook with emotion, her slim frame trembling like a leaf in a storm.

"Well then, you shall have him. I can coerce him, never fear."

"How?"

"I am employed already in embroiling him with the Bishop of Durham. It is not difficult. There is some quarrel between the two already."

"What will you do?"

"I'm not sure as yet. But I have an idea. I think. I see how to bring his pride before a very mighty fall. And, once humbled, I can bargain with him. Yes, that would be it ..." Thomas was deep in his plotting, his hands knotting themselves nervously, his teeth biting at his lower lip. "Yes, I see a way ... a pardon for him, in exchange for some attention to your not-unattractive person ... eh, Chris? How would that suit?"

"What pardon?"

"Until I am sure, I will not say." He limped a step or two away, turning to look at the sun sinking behind the Craignair hills. "But you will not flaunt your success, when you get it?" Thomas suddenly grew softer. "You will not let Dev be harmed? She's ever been good enough to me."

"Oh yes, in her patronising way, she's 'good' to most people. No, you fool. I shall not flaunt Balliol. It would not be prudent, I know that ... scarce even possible."

Thomas the Bastard was tired of his sister's

affairs; they were nothing ... a passing passion. It was his own matters that were of true importance.

"And when our cousin Bruce gives the word, you swear you will let me have money ... and men ... maybe even his backing ... in my claim to the throne of Scotland?"

"Haven't I sworn already?" Christian, too, in her turn, was impatient now with her half-brother's harping. He would never succeed in his ambitious bid ... even if Bruce remained loyal, and did not out-fox him with a bid of his own! But, she could wind Fortibus around her finger, truly enough; and if she could persuade him, as she knew she could, to assist her brother in his wild scheme for wealth and power, all she asked in return was some pressure on Balliol that would make him hers.

"You will finish at the end of some lumpkin's pike, Thomas, if you do not lose your head for plain treason."

"I've more right than you girls," he muttered obstinately. "I am the only male heir. If I cannot be given justice ... I will take it for myself."

"You're a fool," repeated Christian, turning away from Thomas.

"But a fool you'll be glad of yet, madam," he spat out, as he followed her towards the castle, where already, through the slit windows the torch lights began to flare yellow in the summer dusk.

Chapter Four

"I've brought your warmer cloak, my lady." Dervorgilla, pacing the deck of the ship with her husband, looked round to find Kitty holding out a pelisse of fox furs. Gratefully she took it. She had been so absorbed in what Sir John had been telling her about the Ramsey dispute that she had not realised how cold she was now that night had fallen. Standing on the forecastle, high above the rowers, the look-out called his monotonous chant. The wind, even though the year was not yet fully into its fourth quarter, was keen as a knife.

Balliol looked at the plump serving girl. She had been civil enough, but in his own household he would not have permitted a body servant to interrupt him until he had called for him. Too much initiative, like too much salt, went to the head of the lower orders and made them troublesome. But his wife was indulgent in these matters. Well, she had, after all, been brought up in a country fashion; in none of her father's seats was great state kept. When the time came for her to rule Barnard Castle, or, indeed, to set up house in London, things would be different. And she would learn. This lovely Scottish lass was no fool for all her youth and unworldliness. Already

Balliol found it good to talk over with her some of his cares and problems. She knew nothing of statecraft of course, nor yet of the legal aspect of the manifold cares of managing vast estates. But she had a clear view of life which, over-simple though it might be, was often a catalyst to his own more complex considerations. "Thank you Kitty. Is Cecily all right? Is the wet-nurse feeding her enough?"

"Aye, and mair than enough," said honest Kitty. "Ye needna fash aboot the bairn. She's as right as heather."

"I don't know why you needed to bring such a train of people," Balliol said, when Kitty had gone. "You could have left that babe at home with her nurse and her chests of garments, her washing maid and ..."

"Oh but John, I could not bear to leave her. She is very good. And I dote so on her ... I never knew that a baby of one's own was so sweet. I cannot bear to be without her."

"You'll not long be without a babe these many a year yet, if I have anything to say about it!" Balliol replied, with a smile.

Dervorgilla said nothing, but in her heart she was pleased. The blood thrilled in her veins, warming her against the sea air more even than her foxskins could do.

"Tell me again," was all she said. "How soon shall we reach Man?"

"The wind's fair now; if it holds, I think we should sight Ramsey by noon tomorrow. Had we one of the new rudders, instead of the single steering oar which is all your father's ships boast, I would be more certain."

"And you will meet the Abbot when?"

"With all possible haste. Had we not been delayed these two months by your father's illness, it would have been an easier dispute to handle. As it is, waiting will not have pleased the Abbot; as I recall hearing, he was never the most patient of men. Now there will be much need of smooth tongues, flattery, a little palm-greasing here and there ..."

"John, forgive me if I intrude. But, you will hold in your temper when you deal with the Abbot, won't you?"

"I? Temper? Madam, you impugn me."

"No, sire. I do not think I do." A small laugh. "But I know you do not take kindly to the authority of the church; that abbots and such like men bring out your choler."

"And do you wonder? Men should be men ... hard, active. Not sleek pussy-cats forever mimming and mumming. Mother church has much to do here on earth; she needs marry and bury, baptise and shrive us. And let us hope she lays up a pardon for us in heaven. But more than that ...!"

"But Mother church is the seat of learning; of medicine, of all the arts."

"True, my wife ... And so she should be, I'm not saying she shouldn't. But what she shouldn't ... and can't do, is to tell men of affairs, soldiers and statesmen, how to run things. Let her stick to her own line, leave us to ours."

"John, John," under the starlit sky, Dervorgilla shook her head, half-laughing, half-proud of her self-willed lord. "What if the Abbot refuses to parley?"

"He won't. Besides, at the Court of Pleas, in the presence of the King himself, it was admitted that our right was equally as good as that of the Abbot."

"It is better, is it not? The land belonged to my father's first wife, the land and the shore. Surely that encompasses all the fishings?"

"1 believe so. But we will see. Come, sweeting. It is time for bed. We shall know soon enough what my lord Abbot has up his sleeve against us."

♥ ♥ ♥

"It's chilly in here," Dervorgilla said to Kitty.

"What can you expect in such a broken down hovel!" Kitty exploded, with a contemptuous sniff. "Wood ... and rotten at that, in most places; no glazing; a 'garde-robe' for one's private functions where the very guards can hear all that should be between you and your maker alone ... 'tis backward folk they are in this islet, and I'll be gled to get hame to Botel, I can tell you."

"But we're not going to Botel for more than a fortnight. Did I not tell you my aunt, Helen Llewellyn, has bidden us stay with her at

Fotheringhay for this winter?"

"Praise be! That'll warm oor bones a bittie! I'm terrible fond o' my native land but it's gey bleak in the wintertime".

Dervorgilla threw back her head and laughed. "Kitty, Kitty," she remonstrated, gently shaking her head with its golden plaits wound over her ears and the netted silk shining with small brilliants.

At that moment, Balliol strode into the small room. It was clear he was in an ill temper.

"Christ's nightshirt," he fussed. "These churchlings are to be taught a lesson or I'll ..." he paused, at a loss for words.

"What's wrong?" Dervorgilla rose and came to her husband.

"That egg-faced abbot of yours refuses to parley!"

Dervorgilla refrained from pointing out that the Abbot was no more "hers" than anyone else's. A small smile crept about her mouth.

"Sit down, my dear, tell me about it."

"There's nothing to tell." Balliol was purple with fury. "Save that I have declared we will settle the matter by trial of battle!"

This was more serious. "Has he agreed?" Dev asked.

"He has. Moreover he has appointed one Henry le Mareschal, a freeman, to be his champion. I must seek a freeman from among my men. And I have few enough with me. Whoever I choose must be a 'bonny fechter' as you might say; for I must win this contest."

Dervorgilla was silent for a moment, then she said, hesitantly,

"John … do you remember that young man who proved so valiant at the summer tourney? Tall, brown-haired? He carried a green favour in his helmet?"

"mm. By the lord … Robert le Coreer! And he's with me here. And he's a freeman, of equal status. By god, Dervorgilla, you've struck it."

He leaned towards her and kissed her on the brow. His ill-temper had vanished. Dervorgilla thought how mercurial these Normans were – of a hotter blood altogether than the reserved northerners of her native land. Maybe the warmer sun of France did have some effect as Christian vowed it did?

"You're my guiding star," he said. There was something in his voice which showed he was not entirely joking. Dervorgilla felt again that warm sensation of pleasure, as she had when John had called her "sweeting" on the boat.

"The trial is to be on the first fair day," he continued. "Pray that it comes soon for this is hovel enough to lodge in; I would that this were over and we could go. I have a bone to pick with another princeling of the church … Chirkham of Durham. I've kept him waiting. His wrath will be nicely boiling by now … But first we'll teach our friend of Man his lesson."

♥ ♥ ♥

Two days later the mid-September morning dawned fair.

As Dervorgilla was dressing, John came into her room.

"Make yourself as fine as you can," he commanded. "I want the Abbot to feel my power." He himself was splendid in a blue and gold tunic, a deeper blue surcoat over it, and a magnificent red fox cape slung about his shoulders. There was fire in his eyes and he moved restlessly around the small, bare oom.

Watching this virile husband of hers, Dervorgilla thought again how strange it was that, two years ago, they had been virtually strangers to each other. Now, she knew him more closely than anyone else in her life; their babe was the inheritor of their mingled blood ... as the next one would be, if she read aright the signs. And, above all, since she had been married to this great baron, not only had she lost her fear of him but she was drawn more and more to loving him. His mind, his swift grasp of high matters inspired her with confidence; his body thrilled her as a woman. All she asked now was that, perhaps, one day, he might begin to love her, too. Now he had passed from cold indifference, through politeness, to an awakened interest and respect ... perhaps even some small affection. But, she suspected, little more. When he was with her, and particularly if she could help him in any way with his affairs, she won his approval ... his admiration even. But Dervorgilla thought, as her lord left the chamber and she continued with her toilet, there were large areas where they never met on common ground. Domesticity bored Balliol to the point where he scarcely acknowledged that it existed. A great lord's household must run so well that his least whim could be gratified. Children, animals, servants, all must remain in their proper stations and either be seen or not, according to the master's will. As for matters of the soul, Dervorgilla sighed. This was something which troubled her more than she cared to admit, even to herself. John's life was based entirely upon, and bounded by, materialism. His faith was in his own power, wealth, strength. Nothing more. And as yet, Dervorgilla dared not even comment more than passingly on matters of faith. But she must not dawdle now.

"Kitty," she called into the tiny adjoining dressing room where she could hear her maid rustling among the boxes and chests.

"Fetch me my sable cloak; and I will wear my silver gilt filet set with the pearls. And hurry. I have dawdled too long already."

The trial by battle was to take place in a level meadow beside the mill pool of Alington, which was one of the disputed pieces of land between Balliol and the bishop of Man. As the sun came through the yellowing ash trees, Dervorgilla and John rode towards the raised wooden benches which ran along one side of the ground. There was a crowd of serfs, soldiers, peasants, yeomanry, as well as their own ship's crew and all their staff, jostling in ranks outside the ropes which had been erected around the square where the tourney was to take place.

The baron and his lady took their seats not far from the Abbot, who bowed coldly towards them.

There was a stiff breeze which kept the contestants' helmet favours streaming.

The destriers were nervous, pawing at the ground, their white breath pluming in the fresh morning air. The combatant's aides bustled importantly, attending to armour, to the trappings of the mounts, tightening girths, adjusting stirrups. Dervorgilla felt a thrill of excitement. This was small beer compared to the grand jousts she had seen at the English court, but it was, perhaps, that much more thrilling because she was the more personally involved. She knew little of the relative claims of the two sides. How strong a claim did 'custom', which was the Abbot's chief line of attack, have? She did not know. But she was certain that justice would be done and that the winner of the battle would, indeed, be the prover of his master's claim.

The Abbot's man sported his colours of green and white. Robert, their own Balliol man, carried the light and dark blue Balliol colours in his dress. Both men wore armour but that of le Mareschal was old-fashioned and clumsy.

Dervorgilla hoped that neither man would be killed. Each would, doubtless, be scarred in some way, greater or smaller, by today's battle. It was rare for a fatality to occur in trial by strength but it had been known. Dervorgilla, whilst fully conscious of her rights to the disputed fishery, privately considered them too paltry to merit a man's death. Glancing at her husband, sitting stiffly upright, the jewels on his cloak-clasp and on his hands, glinting in the pale sun. With an inward smile she told herself that he would not be entertaining such milk-sop thoughts, she was sure.

A horn sounded at the far end of the field. The crowd fell silent as the two warriors mounted the blocks beside their destriers and with the aid of their helpers, settled between the high pommels of their saddles. Their chain mail glinted. Their vizors were up. Devorgilla thought their own man, Robert le Coreer, looked young and somewhat brittle in comparison with his opponent who was a burly, middle aged Manxman with a smoky face like tanned leather.

The hornblower sounded his instrument again. Now would come the trial by strength.

The silence was complete. All knew that one word uttered during a trial by battle could invoke the penalty of ten cows to be paid to the King ... or their equivalent in hard silver which was none too easy to come by. Both combatants lowered their vizors and urged their horses towards each other.

Slowly at first the two horses moved towards each other. The heavy maces, their iron spheres studded with cruel spikes, swung ponderously before reaching a deadly speed. The combatants crouched low on their mounts, one hand grasping a pommel, the other wielding their weapons faster and faster. The contestants wheeled towards each other, manoeuvering for striking position. The horses grazed each others' flanks for a second. Suddenly le Coreer reined in his horse until his forefeet flayed the haunch of his opponent's beast. Turning with the swiftness of a dancer, Balliol's man struck the Manxman full in his back, unseating him.

… With a mighty bellow of triumph, Balliol jumped to his feet. He turned to where the discomfitted abbot sat, glowering.

"God is with us," Dervorgilla said, rising to stand beside her man.

"And so he should be!" Balliol retorted, grinning. "Did you ever see a face like that …" he inclined his head towards the abbot … "he glooms like a bowl of sour curds!" "Go you to our lodgings, my dear. I must speak with le Coreer; he has done well"

"His wound is not great? Should I not come … or Kate?"

"My dear, our own men know what to do, see, the cook's bringing boiling water now to scald the wound 'ere it festers. He will sew it up neat as a bag pudding. It cannot be much for there's little enough gore. Get you home. I will come for dinner at four o'clock ... not till then for I must order things for our departure. See you that the chests are packed that we may go with the tide tonight."

Chapter Five

The great hall of Fotheringhay Castle in Northampton was a right merry bustle. Helen Llewellyn and her indulgent husband, John le Scot being childless themselves loved nothing more than to have their clansmen around them. Many spent months at a time enjoying their wealthy relatives' hospitality. Some, like Helen's widowed elder sister, made themselves useful in the still room and the linen room. Others, like John's idle youngest nephew, drank his best wines with gusto, spoiled his hawks, lamed his finest mounts and promised imminent reform from season to season, yet lingered always; a peril to the castle maidens and to his uncle's purse.

But John, a burly man of generous instincts and big heart, when scolded by his almost equally indulgent wife, merely shushed her with "He'll grow out of it; he's nought but a lad and ye ken what they're aye like ..."

So now, seated about the great central log fire, this happy pair looked with uncritical eyes at their kin clustered around their Christmas hearth and listened with uncritical ears to the tale of an ancient fighting man newly returned from the holy war against the Saracens. "Holy scuffling," thought le Scot, scratching his over-full belly

contentedly. The wars had been dragging on for
many a generation. Let the infidel keep his
stinking land and let our fighting men attend to
troubles nearer home. France was always an
unchancy bedfellow; there'd be more trouble
there yet. Meantime, let this poor hack earn his
beer and venison with his stuttering tale.

His wife never listenened to these bloody tales
of battle, of sand and heat and flies, of rigours
endured and sores unhealed; they were all the
same. They distressed her, she hated them and
would rather pay the sufferer a groat and bid him
to a warm corner of the hall with the green
youths, to whom his dismal yarns were
something alluring. However, she sat, smiling, to
all appearances listening to the droning fellow,
but her eyes were busy; so were her thoughts.

There was Dervorgilla, growing round, under
her white, fur-trimmed mantle, with her second
babe. She had bloomed with marriage. She had
always been bonny, once past the gawky, over-
fleshed years of adolescence; now she promised
real beauty; by the time she was thirty, thought
her aunt, she would be a regal woman and fitting
wife for her high-handed baron.

She looked at him, standing in the shadows, a
little way off from the hearth. He was flushed
with wine of which, being the festive season,
most of the men of the party, had taken too
much. He would run to fat, thought Helen, but
he was a man to attract and hold women. As he
seemed to attract that brazen minx Christian.

Not for the first time, seeing them together, Helen thought something might be afoot. Now she saw Christian lean back so that her shoulders just touched Balliol's thighs as he stood behind her stool. In the flickering firelight Helen could not be sure how close was the contact; it could have been momentary, innocent. But Helen had seen much of men and women and of passion and lust in her long life. She thought she was not much mistaken that trouble might be brewing here.

"Margaret should have tamed her wanton girl," she thought, unusually severe. There had never been much love between her and her younger sister. A vain, bossy little dumpling.

It was as well she was not here this Christmas; she always stirred someone to retaliation with her commanding tongue. But how was Alan faring? Helen had always liked her gentle Scots brother-in- law. She feared now that his life might be closing. He had been sick for too long and in spite of all that his physician could do, it was becoming clear that his damaged kidneys would never mend; their poison would ooze its way throughout his system. And when that day came, her nieces, Christian, Dervorgilla and her namesake, Helena, would be wealthy in their own right. Would one of them bear a son who might climb to the throne of Scotland when King Alexander died? It was possible. The blood line was there.

The hall rocked with ribald laughter. Helen

left her wandering thoughts. She saw that the crusader had finished his tale and that it was the jester's turn now. In his scarlet and saffron, his cap and bells, he was a droll figure, right enough. And his jokes were fresh. Helen leaned forward to listen with new attention. She liked a good joke, and if it was a bit saucy, well, that was life, after all.

Under cover of the stir of fresh interest among the crowd in the hall, Christian, seeing that her husband, Albemarle was quietly playing draughts with a companion wispy and dullard as himself, insinuated herself closer against Balliol. The fire in her veins was no less since she had been married these four months. Worse, perhaps. Fortibus only managed to stir her desire, not to quench it. She needed a man. And the one man who still tempted her beyond all others was this bull of a man behind her, her own brother-in-law. What had Thomas done yet to ensnare him? Nothing, she dared swear, though she had not seen Thomas this many a day. He would be busy intriguing among his Galloway peasants, no doubt, laying his plans to back Bruce's grab for the Scots crown should Alexander die before his time. Politics! Christian thought, scornfully. They left too little time for the things that mattered. Now she moved her silk-clad shoulders gently, sensually against Balliol's leg, insinuating herself as sleekly as 'Puss-in-the-Corner'.

From half-closed eyes she saw a mud-stained

rider shove his way through the merry crowd and approach behind her uncle's carved oak chair. She saw her uncle incline his silvery head the better to hear the messenger's words. She watched as he spoke to his wife, then rose, raising his hands for silence.

"Pray, silence. We have ill news for Christmas night. Alan of Galloway is dead." All heads bowed for a moment and the Fotheringhay chaplain raised his hand in a quick plea for the soul of the departed, murmuring the prayer for the newly dead. John le Scot's voice grew in volume.

"That is not the worst. His traitor son, Thomas the Bastard has roused Galloway against his sisters, the rightful inheritors of Alan's lands, and, with the connivance of Bruce of Annandale, and backed by the peasants, is even now laying plans to claim the Scot's crown."

There was uproar. Balliol's head cleared of the wine fumes by the shock of the news. That the Bastard would make trouble, somehow, sometime, over something, he had always known; but that he would dare to go so far as to make an open claim as Alan's heir ... this was preposterous. He must go at once. He shouldered his way through the clacking crowd to his wife's uncle, John le Scot. As he strode, he clasped the shoulder of now this one of his knights, now that, bidding them without words, merely by his touch and his look, to don their armour, gather their aides, and prepare for the long journey north.

"I have most of my men at Barnard Castle," he told le Scot. "I will gather them on my way north. You may depend upon it, this upstart will not long hold Galloway."

"I know, I know," John nodded. "Thomas by himself can do little more harm than an angered wasp, dashed from a half-sucked plum; but Bruce of Annandale," the massive grey head shook slowly, "that's another matter. You will need to be well prepared."

"I shall be."

Balliol moved now towards his wife, seated with clasped hands and tear-filled eyes, nearby.

"I must go at once. Do not grieve, Your father was old and very sick. He could have but suffered cruelly. As for Thomas ... well, it may be a stiff fight, but we shall win. Stay here until you hear from me. Helen will care for you." He clasped her lightly about the shoulders.

"John," Dervorgilla answered, inconsequentially, "Wear your warmest cloak. It is bitter indeed. Why, when Helena came from London yesternight she told me that they say the river Thames is freezing over so hard that a man may ride a horse across it."

"God's nightshirt, my love! If nought but frost bite into my bones I shall fare well." One last hand-clasp, one last fond look passed between the two before Balliol left the hall.

♥ ♥ ♥

"Christ," Balliol muttered to his aide, young Guy Dompierre, "I never felt such cold. My very marrow freezes!"

They were riding, on weary horses, now, from Yorkshire, where they had, as Balliol had proposed, collected the bulk of his fighting men, towards the western seaboard of England. They had heard that Bruce and Thomas the Bastard were holding Botel and Kenmure Castles and most of the land between Carlisle and the Urr valley.

On their left, ahead of them, they knew the sea lay not so many miles off but now, through the scarves of dusky mist, they could see little more than a horse-length ahead; there was a faint tang of salt air about them which told them their journey across England's backbone was ended.

"We'll sleep tonight at Arderydd." Balliol looked piercingly at Dompierre. "It's a good two hours' ride from here. Will the men take it? There's a howff there, an inn of sorts, some barns. We'll shelter, though not well."

"They'll do it, sire," the young Norman replied. "And tomorrow we'll cross the Nith at Dumfries; 'twill be a shiversome crossing!" he laughed ruefully, pulling his cloak around him at the very thought of fording the River Nith, with its weir, in such bitter weather.

"If the frost is as hard here as it is in London it may be easier than we think," laughed Balliol. "But 'tis time we'd a bridge. The ferry is alright for the farm folk bringing their hens and their bit corn; but Dumfries grows prosperous; it needs more than a ferry and a ford."

His mind swerved away from the topic to another one.

"Do you know, Dompierre?" he asked, above the jingling of their horses' accoutrements, "they say that hereabouts ..." he waved his right hand vaguely ahead, "King Arthur once lived and died. The great battle was at Arderydd and some say that it was Solway vale he saw as Avalon." His voice grew softer, gentler. "Well, it's fair enough, I warrant, to be any man's Vale of Paradise; I trow I thought Scotland a bearded enough tyke when first I saw her rough stubble; but, as the years go past, I find myself ever happier when I cross into Galloway. True, the wind has a sharper tooth here than in our ancestral land; but Dompierre, when the sun smiles in Galloway there's a beauty to break your heart."

The younger man made no reply. This was a softer side which the Baron had never shown before; Dompierre found it hard to know what to answer. But Sir John seemed lost, now, in a reverie.

They rode on together, their great straggle of men behind them. In the darkening winter evening their armour, their horses' trappings and, now and then, their rough voices, rang harshly against the bitter sky.

♥ ♥ ♥

Balliol was supping a bowl of steaming wine and water, dunking his hunks of barley bread into it as Dompierre came hurriedly into the inn's one, smoke-filled room, early next morning,

"I have news, my lord." the young man said. "Our scouts were out during the night; they picked up a couple of Annandale's men. They say that Annandale and the Bastard are gathering the countryside against us, but that they do not expect us so early."

"They'd expect the weather to hold us back," Balliol said, gobbling fast. "How many are they?"

"I don't know. But the Bruces have a good core of trained soldiers, both spear and archers. Their men said they were collecting all the countryside."

"Well," grinned Balliol, "there's nought to fear there; in the whole of Galloway there'll not be above a handful, you might say." He wiped his black beard on the back of his hand. "Galloway's the emptiest corner of God's earth south of the Bens," he grinned, relishing the thought of the fight to come.

"Do your captives know where the enemy means to stand?"

"They were unsure ... or lying. One spoke of Arthur's Loch ... know you it?"

"Aye. It lies but a few miles west of Dumfries, under the shadow of a small hill. And the other ...?"

"He thinks Thomas will stand at Botel if the Bruce's men have had time to reach it. If not, he thought they would try to hold the narrow plain between the sea and the foot of Criffel." Dompierre hesitated for a moment. "He also said that the men of Galloway were for the Bastard".

"And against the distaff side, eh?" Balliol was quick to pick up the point. "Tis natural. This is a land where men rule and women obey!" He grinned again, then looked serious, "But the inheritance is legally that of the daughters. We cannot allow the Bastard to flout the law."

He stood up, his massive frame filling the low-ceiled hovel. He coughed, in the peat-reek.

"Give me the map," he ordered Dompierre, who produced from his wallet a fragment of sheepskin whereon was drawn an outline of the south of Scotland. Looking at its rough approximations Balliol grinned again, "Our scholars are as wild as our warriors," he said, "When we are firmly in the ruler's seat we must teach them more elegant ways."

Frowning, he studied the plan of the country. Dompierre stood silently by. He knew that the Baron would make his own decision as to the plan of attack and ask for no man's opinion.

"We'll go by the shore road," Balliol said, handing the vellum back to his aide, "We may be able to cut off the Annandale army before they reach Botel and join with the Bastard's gang. If not, we can strike inland, across the country to

Botel. and face them there. Though if they are entrenched in the castle, we'll need siege engines."

He continued, "Tell the guards to tickle the ribs of the two Bruce men with the points of their daggers; find out more news of how many oppose us, what engines they have. Get the troops ready to ride and ride hard, straight for Dumfries."

The mist of the previous night had gone; the day was brilliantly blue but the air was so sharp that every breath caught the throat. Horses and men stamped to warm themselves, and alike they were wreathed in the white plumes of their own breath. Balliol mounted. His hornblower sounded the bugle for silence. He shouted to his followers.

"We shall ride hard for Dumfries. Ford the Nith as you may, once over, follow the shore, keeping behind me as close as you can. At the foot of Criffel, by Kinderloch, I shall halt. The battle may be there; it may be a few leagues on. Do not pass that point and do not tarry. If we can divide the enemy's troops, we shall have an easier victory ... and swifter plunder!"

He wheeled his horse immediately he had finished, and rode off north, Dompierre close behind him, his other aides and lieutenants left to gather up their men, pay for their overnight stabling with a groat or two, and to ride at full speed behind him.

At Dumfries, they galloped in a great,

streaming, jostling cavalcade down the slope leading to the river, The noise of their arrival brought a few rag-padded cottars to the doors of their heather-roofed hovels. But no one cheered. Only the curs yelped hysterically and a bairn or two screamed in terror.

"Curse this soft, western air," Balliol shouted to his aide, as he approached the river bank, "The water is foaming with ice but not solid. We must ford, and it is deep. There'll be belly-ache and fever right enough tomorrow. But see that the men keep on for Kinderloch." He glanced over the river to where the sun glowered like a sulky fire behind banks of grey clouds. "There, we will camp and make fires ... if Annandale is not waiting for us! If he is, then the heat of battle will cauterise their augue!" He wheeled ahead, plunging through the river, below the weir where the dark waters curled savage lips over the grey, sharp teeth of rocks.

His horse quivered and would have turned from the icy water, but Balliol refused to allow it to retreat. Ruthlessly, wet and chilled to the waist, he forged ahead. Arrived on the western bank, he waited until he saw that the army followed him, "Dompierre," he bellowed, "Round up the stragglers. Light fades and we must camp ... or fight ... at Kinderloch. Bid them move their idle bones, for the love of God."

Ignoring his own discomfort and his horse's obvious reluctance to travel much farther or faster that day, Balliol steadfastly proceeded. His mind was busy with the fight ahead. Would he be able to choose the battle site, thus gaining a strategic advantage; would he have to accept a siege of Botel, waiting for siege towers and slings to arrive from Yorkshire, hoping to starve out his brother-in-law's forces? Or pollute their water? His mind ranged swiftly over the structure of Botel. It would be no easy castle to take.

In the thickening gloom, the avengers swept on, out of the soft Nith valley, up and inland, towards the great bulk of Criffel, standing like a sentinel at the gate of Galloway. On the shores of Loch Kinder, they assembled. The weary horses steamed with the heat of their travel, drank among the reeds of the dark loch's edges. The scouts came in to the camp.

"The varlets say that Annandale has not arrived yet, and that Thomas awaits him at the Castle of Wraiths, yonder some five miles, he saw the lights of their fires. They are not so many."

"Good," Balliol said, "Tell the men to boil up their day's huntings, to eat heartily, to sleep quiet, and tomorrow we will attack even before daylight. Keep fires small and make little noise. Doubtless Thomas' scouts will know, if they do not already do so, that we are here. But if they are few, and we take them early, we can scatter them before the Bruce's arrival ... maybe then Bruce, without his ally, will flee ... or parley. Tell the hornblower to arouse the camp at four tomorrow."

Calling for fur rugs, Balliol rolled himself tightly within their comforting embrace, lay close to his horse and slept, soundly, quietly as if he lay beside his lady wife within the ease of his own silken bed.

In the morning ... which yet seemed like the middle of the night, so pitch dark and so icy was it ... no man paused to do more than chomp the last remains of his supper, cold now and grease-encased, to guzzle a crust of hard loaf, to swig from his flask of sour ale. Then, cursing, ill-tempered, stinking, irritable with lice and sweat, hands and feet and noses bone-achingly cold, they gathered in a vast, unwieldy horde, glad to have the excitement of battle ahead.

Balliol and his captains lost no time in starting out towards the sea. Swiftly they rushed towards the wide plain where the ancient Wraiths castle stood. As they approached the salt flats, they could see the crowd of Thomas' army, pin-pointed here and there by a half-dead camp-fire, bulking black against the dawn sky, hear the stomp and snort of horses, the clangour of their bits and bridles, "They are uninformed!" Balliol crowed to Dompierre. "We shall slaughter them as they lie!"

Which is just what they did. In half an hour, the battle's outcome was decided clearly and with no possible doubt. The larger force under Balliol attacked with a merciless ferocity. Thomas' men were scarcely awake 'ere they were struck down with the heavy swords of their attackers. In the dim light they could not tell how many were against them, from which direction they came; could scarcely fumble for their own weapons to defend themselves. It was a massacre.

Not even the least streak of yellow light had arrived to brighten the eastern sky before Balliol's bugles rang out over the sickening scene, calling his men to reform. The fight was ended. Thomas was in shackles and well guarded by two Yorkshire bullies who could put out his puny light as easily as if they crushed a tormenting fly. Most of the Baron's men were still busy dispatching the Bastard's bewildered troops, plundering for food, for weapons, for horses, for anything they could grab.

"Back to Kinderloch," the captains were crying. And, more or less, that was where the victors reassembled. It took some more than the morning to wander back, drunk on the beer, the wines they had found in Thomas' camp; some had stopped to slake their lust among the camp-followers. Some joined their captors willingly enough. Victors had fires and food; they had daggers they could barter to the countryfolk for hens, or turnips; sometimes they had extra plaids and woollens which they might give to their trollopes; anything was better than being left alone, penniless and foodless, to wander through the winter land, begging for scraps, scavaging with the dogs among the refuse piles about the cottage doors.

Balliol's men had erected a stout tent. Which

was as well for now the sullen morning had broken into lashing rain. Beyond the shore, the waves of the Solway waters were wild.

Balliol stripped off his clothes and rubbed himself with a coarse linen towel before putting on the clean linen, the only-slightly damp tunic, the warm surcoat and a dry cloak lined with bearskin. The brazier held glowing peats; his servants were setting a camp table for him and from outside, in the gloomy afternoon, came a smell of stewing meat.

His captains began to arrive; each, though weary, was warmly clad, refreshed in spirit by their speedy victory, easy that they could sleep that night more comfortably than for the past week, not too anxious for the other half of the enemy, which still waited to be put down. Balliol was in high humour. He drank spiced ale from a metal beaker.

" 'Twas easier than I'd expected," he told his commanders. "And tomorrow's fight against the Bruce will be as simple. The land is ours."

"But the people?" began one of his lieutenants, "They favour the Bastard's cause? May they not rise for him even yet?"

"No," said Balliol. And there was nothing of the braggart in his confident monosyllable. "These people are half-wild. Without a leader, they can do nothing. They are scattered across the land in ones and twos. There is no army, other than those poor devils we routed this morning. If we can show Annandale the edge of our swords as we did the Bastard, then we may return to our families with easy minds. Come, let us eat. We can plan as we fill our bellies with hot food. But I tell you, victory is as easily ours tomorrow as if we took a child's toy from him while he slept."

♥ ♥ ♥

The Baron was right. The next day, in the continuing rain, it was merely a question of turning about, and facing the small force of Annandale warriors who came along the shore road to meet what should have been their ally's troops, and there, under Criffel's leaden hump, to dispatch the greater part of them almost as easily as Balliol had prophesied.

The chaotic scrabbling for loot, the swift dispatch of the wounded, of shrieking nags, the grabbing of anything one wanted and could hold against one's comrades' greed ... all was over in a few hours. Some of the men of Durham and York were only too thankful. They loathed the wild shore, the rude hills, the treacherous bogs of the country they found themselves in.

"Fight to keep this wilderness?" they asked each other with hearty scorn. "Let the wolves and the ravens have it. Thank God we belong to a civilised region. The sooner we get back home the better. This is Devil's land. Wonder what the old man sees in it?"

But the old man saw plenty. He was well

content … almost disappointed that the enemy had offered such little opposition.

But he saw ahead a golden age. Galloway would be shared now between his wife and her sisters. Together he and Dervorgilla would rule their portion. Vague thoughts of the close link with the Scots crown and how this might work to their advantage in the years ahead passed through his mind. But now, he was more interested in ideas he had discussed lately with his wife for the draining of some of Galloway's bogs; if they could do this, then, surely, crops could grow here, cattle be reared? Not so easily as in his lands in Picardy, nor yet so fruitfully as his Yorkshire acres; but no land was without hope. Balliol sighed with pleasure, with relief, with the healthy weariness of a man who has put his latest battle behind him. Men spoke of him as a battling baron; but they did not fully know him who spoke thus.

Battles must be fought; fought and won, because until they were, progress could not be made. And this was the age of progress; the golden age, when learning and commerce, when law and new ways of working the land should reap a golden harvest.

Thank God he had married a woman with a mind, a woman who could help him administer and improve their lands.

"Send Dompierre to me," he presently told a page.

And when his aide came, he said,

"Take the Bastard to Durham. There put him in the dungeon. Then join me at Fotheringhay. The last of the Christmas feasting will not yet be done." His red lips gleamed beneath his black moustache.

"There will be venison, and pasties; mincemeat well spiced. There will be minstrels. And dancing. Don't delay in joining us there."

And as Dompierre left the tent, John Balliol thought 'us' ... and the 'us' of his dreams was himself, his beautiful wife, their pretty babe ... and the son who would, surely, soon be born to them. He would found a dynasty. The absolute power over his own Norman holdings, his English acres, his wife's inheritance of this wild land of heather and rock ... her expectations of lusher pastures in Northampton when her aunt Helen died ... these were fine and enough to be going on with.

But they were only a beginning. Much lay ahead. As he unbuckled his sword and cast off his surcoat, John Balliol dreamt of fortune, power ... of fame echoing down history's brightest corridors ... these thoughts wove a golden curtain of happy dreams in which he wrapped himself, rich in fact, richer yet in anticipation.

Chapter Six

The man's great bull's roar of laughter rang through the garden where the bees hummed about the catmint border.

"God's doublet, sweeting, you should have been one with Heloise! A scholar ... a woman with a mind of her own!"

"Don't say that, John," Dervorgilla spoke almost nervously.

"My love, why ever not?"

"Their's was not a happy story. I ... I don't want you to speak of them in the same breath as us ..."

Balliol looked, unusually serious, at his wife's lovely face.

"And ours is?" he asked. "A happy story?"

Dervorgilla laid down the silk tapestry she was stitching.

"Oh yes, my darling," she said, fervently, taking her husband's hands in her own. "A truly happy story. We are much blessed."

Gently Balliol leaned towards his wife and kissed her. "You did not always think so," he returned to his teasing note. "You would have refused me ... and hied yourself ..."

"Don't say 'to a nunnery'," Dervorgilla broke in.

75

"I should not have liked that. But oh," she breathed rapturously, clasping her hands excitedly, "how I should have loved to be a 'poor scholar' at one of the new colleges of learning which the Black and Grey Friars are beginning to build at that village west of London ... the one whose name I always forget."

"You mean Oxford, my love."

"To hear from the lips of men who may personally have known the gentle St. Francis, stories of his wonderful ways of dealing with animals and men. To learn the courses of the stars, the wisdom of government ... all the knowledge that the world has gathered through the long centuries."

Balliol was growing bored. "You could never have been, never could be, a 'poor scholar', my love. You are a great woman; a woman of wealth and power. It is better. You may reach the thousands by your rule and your management. Worth far more than mumping in some cobwebby corner over old parchments."

He stood up, stretching his long limbs as he spoke. Dervorgilla stood beside him, "John," she said, picking up her tapestry and preparing to return to the castle. "I want to ask you. For a long time ... ever since, in fact, you told me of the icy Nith crossing you were forced to make when you put down my brother's rebellion ... I have thought that it would be a fine thing if we were to build a bridge there, at Dumfries. I should like to build a fine, arched bridge across which my people of Galloway could mingle with their southern brethren. And I have thought, too, that I should like to endow a small community of friars somewhere close to the White Sands. They could do much for the townfolk; Dumfries grows yearly and yet remains unsavoury, unhealthy ... and the people have no teaching for their young ones. Could we not establish a small monastery close by the banks of the river? The Grey Friars could take the tolls from the bridge, could plant orchards by the river and could make a small hospital and a school, and we ..."

"Angels wings!" Balliol broke in. "You have it all worked out, have you not? I daresay you have even asked the masons for plans and your bailiff for costs?"

"Oh no, not quite yet. I wanted to see if you would agree first."

"Well, my love, I do. I do. See you to it, and when the plans are ready in detail, I will look at them and you shall give your bridge to Dumfries. But now, my belly growls; I'm sure it is the dinner hour ... and I want to see my children before I eat.

As the Lord and Lady of Balliol reached the oaken door in the south tower of Botel Castle, they could hear an appalling hullabaloo.

John Balliol thrust open the door and stood, legs spread, hands on hips, gazing with quizzical eyes at the melee.

Kate, grown stouter and greyer, held a baby of

eighteen months astride one hip; her face was red with annoyance as she flapped a linen napkin at the two girls who were tormenting Tam, the terrier, grown, like Katie, to own a sprinkling of grey amongst the tawny hairs of his rough coat.

"Nay, Marjory, be still," Kate cried. "Sit down and leave the pup."

"Pup!" Marjorie shrieked ... "He's no pup; he's as old a ... as ..."

Cecily, the taller of the two girls, busy trying to drag a rag doll from the terrier's mouth, suddenly caught sight of her father blocking the doorway. At once, she grew quiet, dropped a curtsey and turned to join her brother Hugh where he sat at the meal table, dipping his hunk of bread into the gravy which had collected in the rim of his wooden platter from the stewed hare crowning it.

Kate, too, suddenly became aware that the Baron was paying one of his rare visits to the nursery and with a hiss of command to the rumbustious Marjory, small and dark, and comically resembling her father, she, too, dropped a quick curtsey.

Balliol strode into the small room where rough wooden toys littered the rush-strewn floor and where a young nurse-maid was filling a tub with hot water. Clean nightshirts were draped on stools and benches near the small fire.

The big man took the baby from Katie.

"Well, Alexander, my newest son, " he said, tossing the bairn into the air and hearing him crow with half-frightened glee. "You grow apace, and you'll not be the bairn o' the brood much longer," he added, glancing at his wife's rounded silhouette.

Dervorgilla spoke to Kate.

"How is he? How are they all?'

"Healthy as heather, my lady. The wee one's tearing all over the place. I canna keep pace with him."

"He's a true Yorkshireman," beamed Balliol. The three older children had all been born in Scotland but Alexander had arrived when Dervorgilla had spent a winter at Barnard Castle and John liked to tease his wife about having an English son.

John gazed at his brood with pleasure. Cecily was tall for a girl of ten, but a trifle too pale; but so much like her mother that her father held a particular affection for her. Hugh, his first-born son had the fiery hair and white cheeks which flame throughout Galloway among the dark curls and the lint locks of their siblings. But Hugh was bookish; this was something his father scarcely understood ... no doubt he got it from his mother's side ... old King David had been something of a scholar and a saint. They would have to make Hugh an abbot, if he did not soon take more to hawking and sword-play.

"But this boy," he said, allowing his thoughts to rise into speech, "he bears a king's name. and he'll have the bearing of a king." He tossed young Alexander towards the ceiling again.

"Aye, he's a knight; a warrior, I'll forecast."

Dervorgilla, seated on a low chair beside the table, talking quietly with the elder children, her hands caressing the little terrier, who had come thankfully to her side and was licking her fingers with affection, smiled at the picture her husband made with their small son; they were alike in all save colouring; sturdy, demanding, lusty with life … Alex would be a warrior right enough … a great leader of men …

She was roused from her daydreaming by Katie's voice saying quietly in her ear.

"And are you carrying well this time, lassie?"

"Oh yes." Dervorgilla smiled at her old companion and serving maid who now ruled the nursery. "I'm never better than when I'm with child. It suits me."

"Aye," Katie murmured. "I'm thinking married life suits you …" her eyes went approvingly to the great Baron playing with his son. "I had my doubts, in the early days. But you were made for life, for love, for bairns. And ye've a guid man, I'll say that."

Dervorgilla's eyes shone like emeralds. Silly, how she warmed to Kate's approval of 'her man', but Kate had been her earliest and closest friend and mentor, and besides, Kate was as sound and sane as it was possible to be, and her approval was not lightly given.

"Kate," Devorgilla said. "I want you to leave the children in the care of young Mattie when we reach Fotheringhay and be with me yourself until the new child is born. Can you do that?"

Katie looked doubtful for a moment, plucking at her lower lip with one hand even as she unthinkingly, of custom, shovelled a spoonful of bread and gravy into Marjory's unwilling mouth with the other; she looked at the girl who was airing the two youngest children's night-wear. Then she smiled, "I think she'll do. Besides, your aunt has plenty servants and we can pick a good lass to help Mattie. And, between times I can keep an eye on the young monkeys. When do we go south?"

"Next week," Dervorgilla said. "Aunt Helen's lonely since my uncle died. And from there it will be easier for my lord to attend to affairs of state. They say there may be war with Gascony soon." Dervorgilla sighed. The one flaw in her deep happiness with her husband was the fear that he might be slain in some battle. Henry of England never ceased stirring up trouble in France and as one of his most powerful barons, John must be continually ready to defend the king's interests.

Balliol broke into her thoughts by depositing Alexander back in Kate's arms. He tousled the heads of the other three youngsters, saying, "Come, my dear; I am hungry. The goslings have their beaks full ... 'tis time for their parents to appease their pangs."

Before leaving the room where the dusk was already casting shadows in the corners, Balliol spoke to Kate.

"Look after them well, nurse. They are our

hope for the years ahead." Then his seriousness passed as he added, "And make sure my lady's brought to bed of a boy again this next time. 'Tis well to make sure of the line when there's so much to secure."

Kate thought of her master's words a week later when Dervorgilla lay, asleep at last, in the great bed of her room at Fotheringhay.

The birth of her new babe, a puny girl, born two month's too soon, had given her mother more trouble than any of the previous four children. Travelling too near her time, Katie thought, smoothing her hair. Thank heaven the mid-wife had been already waiting, for this last birth had been more than Kate, unaided, could have managed. The household should have moved south a month earlier but Dervorgilla and John so loved Botel, set in its rounded, forest-covered hills within glimpse of the Firth of Solway, that they were always loath to leave it, even for the warmer weather and greater luxury of Fotheringhay.

Ah well, please God the babe would live, even though it was a girl and frail, and not looked upon with any great favour by her father, at least.

Balliol had been distraught by his wife's hard labour and intensely thankful when it was safely over but on being shown the baby had said sadly to Kate,

"God's shoon, Kate, three lassies? 'Tis too many. I cannot put lassies into armour to fight my cause and keep my lands safe."

"Mayhap she'll marry well," Kate had ventured, trying to offer some comfort to dispel the Baron's disappointment.

"Mayhap," the man had answered, moving away, not interested in the future of this daughter.

He had gone into his wife's room then. Kneeling beside the bed, he'd kissed her hands. She opened her green eyes, soft as river-shadows and clouded a little still, with the last of the pain which, this time, had been almost unbearable.

"Sweeting," he said, quietly. "It's past. I thank our God that you are safe delivered of this child. But my heart was heavy at the cost." He bowed his dark head for a moment, struggling with his emotion.

Dervorgilla only smiled a little. Then, in a tired voice she said,

"I know she is not what you would have had, John. But perhaps the next one will be another boy. All babies are gifts from heaven. You will come to love her as I do already, when you see her grow and become bonny."

"Yes, my love, yes I shall. After all, she's from your flesh and mine, grown from the love we hold for each other." He kissed his wife's hands again, then stood up.

"I must go now to Barnard. Bishop Chirkham is harrying my men about a disputed boundary. See that Kate takes good care of you and when you are fully recovered, I shall be here again. And then we must to Picardy, for there's a matter of some forest land to be settled there. May God guard you, sweeting."

Dervorgilla raised herself against the fine white linen pillows filled with eider-goose down.

"John," she said, "You have spoken more than once lately of Bishop Chirkham. Is there some trouble brewing? You've long harried each other but I feel there is something more ..."

"Don't fret yourself, my heart. His men have dared to dispute a piece of wasteland with mine, 'tis all. I'll settle it once for all, quickly enough. And be with you before even you've risen from childbed." He bent and kissed Dervorgilla, holding her close, kissing her deeply, tenderly, but without passion. As he smelt her faint perfume of herbs and fresh linen his senses stirred. Ten years back he could not have believed how this slender, serious girl would have twined herself close to his heart, so that whenever he was away from her he felt as if a part of his own core were missing. He smiled into her eyes, noting the mantling of red in her cheeks in response to his own quick-kindling desire. God's beard, but she was a woman above all others!

"'Twill not be long," he said, saluting her from the door of her chamber.

♥ ♥ ♥

And Balliol was right. It was not long until he returned to his wife, where she was as yet barely recovered from little Ada's birth.

Dervorgilla was sitting at her chamber window

in the early afternoon, a bed-gown of deep blue brocade, edged with marten fur, around her. She was still pale from her recent labour. She sat now, with two of her ladies helping her, embroidering a panel of tapestry showing the infant Jesus playing at his mother's feet. The late summer sounds of bees, of doves, of birds practising their migratory flight mingled with the calls of the children on the playing-green below. One of the ladies was reading a tale of knightly love from a handsomely decorated book. She broke off as the children below set up a shouting through which could be heard the jingling of horses' harnesses, the shout of male voices and a scurrying from the direction of the great gate.

"I think some travellers have come," Kate said to her lady Dervorgilla. "It must be someone … or something of importance for there is a great to-do."

Dervorgilla paled then flamed. "Go quickly," she commanded, laying a hand imploringly on Kate's arm … "Perhaps it is my lord himself returned early." In the excitement of the moment she looked like a young girl again.

"Oh no, madam," spoke the younger woman. "Why, he could scarce have ridden to Yorkshire and back in the time, leave alone attended to his affairs."

"Yes, you are right," Dervorgilla smiled. "I am foolish. But when the heart wills … sometimes the mind falls under the spell, too."

Even as she spoke there was the sound of swift

footsteps outside the door. Balliol burst into the room. He was covered in dust, hot, tousled and clearly under some distress.

Dervorgilla said to her companions, "Leave us now. Adela, see that we are not disturbed. And send hot water, towels and some wine by a quiet page."

She rose, leaving her tapestry frame by the window and as the last of the ladies left, she took her husband in her arms.

"My lord," she murmured. "You come in sore trouble, I see it in your face. Come, cast off your cloak, your surcoat, sit here and tell me what is wrong." Lovingly, quietly, her eyes watched him. She had rarely seen her husband look thus. His eyes were red-rimmed with fatigue, the lines of his cheeks and beside his nose were carved deep and his mouth was set as if he clenched his teeth to bear pain.

"Aye," he said, sinking into a chair. "This is bad news. I need your counsel, Dervorgilla and your support as never before."

With the intuition which comes of love, Dervorgilla guessed.

"Chirkham?"

"Yes."

The page came in, put down the bowls, the linen towels, the pewter flagon he bore on the tray and went out quietly. Dervorgilla helped her husband to relax, poured wine for him into a goblet, bathed his face with the herb-scented water.

After a few moments John spoke. "I have fallen foul of his mightiness. Lord, but he's an arrogant pipkin!" He sighed. "But he means to cause me great trouble. Already he has informed the King that I have trespassed into his territory."

"But John ... these squabbles over boundary lines ... they go on all the time. You need not fear Henry's wrath for such a little ..."

"My love. Wait. This is more than a mere land scuffle. Only wait a moment and I will tell you the whole story."

Dervorgilla seated herself on a gilded bench, taking her husband's left hand in hers, and waited quietly while he spoke.

"My steward Rolf," he said, "had my orders to torment Bishop Chirkham's men somewhat until the dispute over our marching lands should be resolved by the king. But the bishop's men took Rolf and his band one night and held them captive. In revenge Rolf laid wait for the Bishop's party as it went out from Durham Cathedral a week or two later and, by the Devil's chance, they captured the band they had laid the ambush for ... but among them was Chirkham himself ... the arrogant Walter, no less!" Balliol laughed, shortly, harshly.

Dervorgilla watched him with her loving eyes but all her courage could not hide the alarm in them.

"Did they ... did they harm the Bishop?"

"Aye. That they did. They rolled him in the

dust. They bound him with cords. They bade him walk before them back to Durham ... that fat lard-tub, walking!"

"Oh John! But did they not know 'twas his holiness?"

"Rolf swears not. But even claiming the cloak of night, he must have had his suspicions. But Rolf is not a man with too much love for the pomp of the clerics ... like myself," John added, with a flash of honesty.

"Chirkham, of course, insists that not only did Rolf know full well whom he had taken prisoner, but that he took him, and humiliated him, at my express command. He has told the king this. I saw Bishop Walter myself yesterday morning and he was puffed like a toad with wounded pride. I offered him all the disputed lands plus half an acre more inside the boundary. But he would not listen. It's revenge he wants."

"And he will get it," breathed Dervorgilla. "Mother church cannot be flouted. Oh John, you have made a grave error."

"I admit it, my heart, I admit it. What am I to do?"

"What can you do?"

"Little enough. I thought of raising the county and settling the matter by force of arms."

"Not against the Church! Not even your power could withstand that!" Dervorgilla was chalk-white with shock.

"I know, I know ..." The big man shook his

head. "But be sure he will demand ... or make the king demand some fearful reparation."

♥ ♥ ♥

Dervorgilla sat erect, her back stiffer than any rod of iron. From her seat in the centre of the flag-bedecked wooden stand, facing the Cathedral in Durham, she looked over the scene. The crowds were enormous, the sultry air was filled with their intense excitement. Her mind went back to that year ... so long ago it seems now ... when as a new bride with her husband in a smaller crowd than this, she watched the trial by battle when another dispute with the clergy had been settled ... that time, in her favour. But this was something much bigger, much more serious.

This was no trial. And the crowds knew it. This was a scene such as few of them were ever likely to see repeated; a public humiliation of one of England's greatest men, at the hands of one, less powerful in his own right, but awe-inspiring by virtue of the enormous authority of the Church whose appointed prince he was.

Dervorgilla sat alone save for Kate and a page. Her heart surged like the sea within her bosom but she kept a hold on herself which was royal in its intensity. Not for nothing was she a descendant of the Scottish royalty, not for nothing was she the wife of a Norman baron whose own standards of discipline and bearing in times of stress were of the highest.

She knew that some of the nobles and their ladies who filled the benches above and below her, and the church dignitaries and courtiers who sat not far from either side of her were not ill-pleased to see Baron Balliol brought to book. Some, it is true, were murmuring against the king for having allowed the Bishop of Durham to go so far in his revenge; what could happen to Balliol today could, all too easily, fall upon them tomorrow. But Balliol was too wealthy, too powerful, too arrogant not to attract no little jealousy from his peers. Dervorgilla's cheeks burned but she turned her head neither to right nor to left; only gazed before her, her green eyes blazing like a tiger's. Whatever he had done, however foolish, or braggart Balliol had been in allowing ... even in urging ... his retainers to tweak the Bishop's nose ... by her bearing she signalled to the onlookers her perfect loyalty, her absolute confidence in and love for the man whose appearance they all awaited.

The autumn day had begun with an unseasonable heat; now, in the midday glare from a yellow sun, insects danced, gluttonishly fastening on the sweaty skin of the serfs whose unwashed bodies emitted a sickening stench, where they herded together on the sides of the square which lay bleached as a chessboard before the Cathedral steps. Behind them could be heard the hoarse cries of the sweetmeat sellers, the purveyors of salt pork and hard bread, the huckster cries of the vendors of fairings.

"A Roman holiday indeed, lassie," Katie ventured to whisper to the stony profile beside her. But the lady Balliol made no answer.

She was watching where now, through the Cathedral's lofty doors, came the Bishop, in procession. His much-embroidered and bejeweled robes glinted in the sun. A man of small stature, the bulk of his most ritual garments squared him to a height no more than his width; his face flamed with pride, with arrogance. He waddled to the top of the Cathedral steps, his retinue spreading themselves like some great barrier, on either side of him,

"Dear God," thought Dervorgilla, "does he think that even now John may affront his person, attack his property?" For a moment she almost could have smiled at the absurdity of the notion, then she was aware that from the heavily guarded tent placed some twenty feet in front of the lowest Cathedral step, a lone figure was slowly emerging.

The quick tears sprang to her eyes as she watched her husband move, head erect, shoulders set firmly, with deliberate paces, from the tent towards the Cathedral with its waiting group.

Even in his bare feet, his tunic of brown hessian, with his head uncovered and his great wrists shackled behind him with rope, John Balliol had all the majesty and power of a nobleman. The crowd murmured in admiration as they watched him, his jaw firmly set, his eyes boldly fixed upon Walter Chirkham, waiting, gloating, at the top of the stone steps.

Unhurriedly, Balliol moved to the foot of the steps. Unhurriedly, he mounted them, moving proudly and with absolute composure. In the background a cheer rang out, then another; but they were hushed as the Bishop's guards, thickly posted among the crowd, dug the ribs of the offenders.

Now the Baron stood two steps below the Bishop. The one in his stark garb looked like the avenger, so proud, so strong did he appear; the other, for all his gold thread and jewels, looked like some circus jester, squat, commonplace and gaudy.

The tears cleared from Dervorgilla's eyes. In her pious heart she admitted that John had done wrong. But in the very innermost fibre of her being she thrilled to him now, splendid in time of degradation as never before.

Bishop Chirkham waited for John Balliol to take the next step towards him, where their eyes were on a level.

In a shrill voice, thin with spite, tense with the lust for triumph over the powerful man who had too long been a thorn in his flesh, Walter Chirkham called to two henchmen:

"Strip him!"

With vicious relish, the two men ripped the coarse tunic to Balliol's waist, exposing the mighty torso with its covering of virile hair, to the crowd's gloating, greedy eyes. Dervorgilla felt as if the pain and humiliation were her own.

Balliol flicked not an eyelash but stood, stiff as a pillar, his dark eyes fixed ... mockingly? ... upon his tormentor.

The Bishop drew himself up to his trifling height and shrilled out again :

"Kneel!"

Still gazing at the toad-like figure before him, Balliol knelt.

For a third time, the voice squealed out:

"Lay on!"

The two henchmen stepped forward once more. This time they held in their hands leather whips. The short, thick handles sprouted a cascade of knotted, leather tails, 'water soaked' the better to bite into human skin and flesh.

In the dusty sunlight, on the steps, above the crowd, silent now, their ghoulish concentration punctuated only by the croak of two ravens which circled above the square, the two men raised their flails and brought them, with a sickening whistle, ending in a staccato of bites, across John Balliol's bare back.

Dervorgilla shut her eyes, reached for Kate's hand and fought the waves of nausea which rose inside her. Slowly, the tears rose to her eyes, and unchecked, coursed down her ivory cheeks.

"There, there, ma doo, dinna fash, dinna fash," Katie murmured, almost crushing her lady's hand with the vehemence of her own red paw, willing comfort and strength to flow through it into her mistress' grieving heart.

Dervorgilla opened her eyes. If she kept them closed, as she longed to do, she would be betraying her beloved John, giving him less of herself than she should ... or would. She forced her chin to stay high, forced her lips to remain steady.

The seconds dragged on as if they had been centuries. Would this agony never cease. The blood showed now across the powerful shoulders of her husband. Imploring in her heart that this torment should cease, she gazed at the now puce face of the Bishop. She saw him thrust a tongue tip out and lick his lips; would he never signal his men to cease their work?

Now! The overloaded, squat figure of the man of God raised a white, pudgy hand. For the last time his effeminate voice pierced the heavy air:

"Enough!"

As his men let fall their whips, Chirkham addressed his victim.

"Nevermore flaunt the power of Mother Church, Baron Balliol. Or you will feel again a weight upon your shoulders."

The Bishop turned, abruptly. His retinue fell in behind him. He vanished back into the great stone edifice from whence he had issued ... ten minutes ... ten aeons ago.

The two brutes hauled Balliol to his feet. His head was still high. He moved back towards the tent. As he went, his dark eyes, expressionless now, fighting the stinging biting pain, met those of his wife.

A smile, faint, but true, passed between them.

Chapter Seven

"Mother," Hugh said, sighing and slouching wearily at the desk, "why must I learn French? I'm a Scot."

"But your father is a French land-owner, first of all; long before he became a man of estate in England, or one of' the nobles of Scotland, he, and his ancestors were powerful land-owners in Picardy. You know all this. Come now, son, just half an hour longer."

"But, Mother," the boy fidgetted on the hard bench, his fingers wandering idly over the parchment before him, his eyes straying to the narrow window, beyond which he could see the far hills stretching away to Kirkcudbright, "I shall begin lessons properly with my tutor after the New Year. Why must I swot now?"

"Hugh! you are already eight years old; you are our oldest son, the one who will inherit all our wealth. How can you administer your father's Norman properties if you cannot speak French?"

Hugh sighed again.

"I don't want to be a great baron, a man of wealth and power. That means moving all the year long from castle to castle, it means dealing justice out to wrong-doers, being in the King's

counsel, and I think that can be bad,
sometimes," he said, a suddenly acute look
making him look older, in spite of his babily-
pudgy cheeks and innocent eyes.

"I'd much rather be a scribe ... or a minstrel,"
he said, brightening with the sudden mood-
swing of the young.

"My darling boy," Dervorgilla said, laughing
softly and running her hand through her son's
fine hair, "these are dreams." She leaned her
wimpled chin on her hand and her eyes grew
dreamy; "But I used to think like you. I'll tell
you a secret, Hugh. I didn't want to marry and
be a great lady, commanding a family, ordering
her affairs first in one home, then in another."

"What did you want to be then?"

"Well, once I thought of being a nun, where I
could nurse the sick, help the poor, study the
lives of the saints." She gave a deprecatory laugh.
"But, truly my son, had I not married your father
and become your mother, I should have liked
best of all to be a scholar at Oxford and later,
perhaps to have written fine books." Her eyes
suddenly sparkling, she straightened herself,
patted the lad on his cheek and said,

"So you see, sweeting, I understand how you
feel. Just as much as I know what can and cannot
be for you. Come now, Hugh, we must work a
little more before the sconces are lit. A boy has
much to learn these days. It is not like your
ancestors' days when to fight and to hunt, to rule
by rough justice were the lessons a nobleman

learned. Nowadays, in this wonderful age of learning, a man of high degree must know much of all these things, but something too, of the new sciences, of chemistry and of the winds and the weather, of politics, of statecraft; the world grows smaller and we must learn much if we are to live at peace with our neighbours. You must know the laws of England, of Scotland and of France; then, too, you must learn, later on, something of Latin, something of a courtier's ways, of music ... falconry ... archery ..."

"Oh mother, stop! You make my head spin," the boy cried, pulling her hand to him and kissing it.

From the neighbouring chamber came a sound of high pitched shrieks.

"The others do not work," Hugh pouted.

"They have been working," his mother replied reasonably. "Cecily has not long finished with me in the still-room, Marjory has her ABC by heart already ... and would you have Alex at two and Ada not yet a year apply themselves to some skill? Nay, my heart," she laughed. "Their turn to study and to work will come soon enough; let us not waste more time in idle discussion. Now ... the verb 'tenir', please ... all the way through."

Hugh saw that his mother was not prepared to indulge him longer. Outside, the early dusk of late autumn was filled with a strange luminosity; the sea mist was rolling up the valley again. It was eerie. It made him think of the ghosts which the serving men said came in the mist to trouble mortals. Hugh was very afraid of such apparitions although he'd never seen one. Better to fill one's head with awkward, tongue-screwing French than to let one's heart be chilled by the thoughts of ghosts and all they might do.

As he bent to scratch awkwardly on the parchment with his pen, there came a particularly prolonged and urgent bout of yelling from the play-room next door.

Dervorgilla rose. "Continue, Hugh, until the sconces are lit," she said. "I must see what those girls are doing."

"Kate," she said, as she entered the play-room "What are you about to allow so much ...?" But Kate was not to be seen and in the half-light, filled with the flickering from the logs in the iron basket resting in the chimney piece, she could see her two elder daughters struggling together. They wore some kind of make-shift helmets on their heads; odd pieces of cast-off armour, it looked to be, tied on their curls with leather thongs. The same odd assortment of metal pieces adorned their chests. In their hands they brandished wooden swords. As Dervorgilla stood, unobserved and unheard in the melee, she heard Marjory cry,

"You shall die, bastard."

And with the words she hurled her strong little body at her taller, though more finely drawn, sister, sending her clattering to the floor with a sound of falling metal more suited, thought Dervorgilla, her lips twitching with amusement, to the kitchen quarters than to the play-room.

Marjory plumped herself squarely on her vanquished sister's chest "Give yourself up bastard-born-on-the-top-of-the-blanket!" she said with vigour.

Dervorgilla could contain herself no longer.

"What did you say, Marjory?" she said, interrupting the children and hauling them to their feet.

"I'm playing father, vanquitching Uncle Thomas," the sturdy lass declared, facing boldly up to her tall mother.

"Vanquishing," Dervorgilla said, automatically. "But what do you lassies know of your Uncle Thomas?"

Cecily, always less forward than her younger sister said, slowly removing her breast-plate with fingers that stumbled over the knotted leather strings,

"That he lies in prison at Barnard for trying to fight our father. And ..." she ducked her head in embarrasment, "that he was born ... not on-top-of-the-blanket, like that ninny says," ... she jerked a chin at Marjory ... "but that he was born under a blanket ... something about a blanket, anyway," she finished helplessly. "Mama ..." in a rush of curiosity, "people speak of him as Thomas the Bastard. What is it ... a bastard, I mean?"

Dervorgilla sat down on a rush-bottomed

chair and drew her lassies to her. Encircling them, in the quiet fire-light, she said,

"What you two chicks are trying to say is something which the serfs say when they speak of someone who is a bastard ... the phrase is 'born on the wrong side of the blanket' and that is the same as saying born out of wedlock."

"I don't understand," said Cecily, puckering her forehead.

"In the old days," their mother continued, "it was no sin for one's mother and father not to be wed. Indeed, until only a few hundred years ago, a hand-fast wedding was all that anyone required. But since this land became Christian, after St. Ninian built his White House at Whithorn, Mother Church and the law of all civilized people, say that it is right for a woman and a man to be married only in church. Only that way can law and order be maintained. And only the children of such a marriage can receive the property and lands of their parents when they die. But, sometimes," Dervorgilla continued more slowly, wondering just how much these young ears should, or could be told, "Men and women ..." she searched for a suitable word, "wed without going to church. And then their children are not their children in law, they are only their natural children. Do you under-stand?"

The bairns nodded. Cecily was all attention; she had reached the age when all matters concerning the two sexes exerted an irresistible draw upon her. Marjory was less interested. She began to fidget.

"Your Uncle Thomas was the son of your grandfather, Alan of Galloway, by a hand-fast wedding made with a country lass.They say she was very beautiful."

"Where is she now?" Cecily asked.

"She died when Thomas was born," Dervorgilla said. "And it was well for her. For until a few years back, the church was very hard upon unwed mothers. They bore their children in shame. Then their children were scorned by all church-going, well-doing folk."

"Is that why Uncle Thomas is in prison?"

"No. During these past twenty or thirty years, with the coming of wider learning from the Continent, and the teachings of gentle Christians such as St. Francis, many of us have come to think that to be born a bastard is not the fault of the baby and that it should not suffer."

"Then why is he in prison?" said Marjory, persistantly. She didn't really understand all that Mama was telling them, but she'd once peeped into the door leading to the dungeons at Barnard Castle and the thought of that dark, dreadful place fascinated her.

"Your Uncle Thomas was a poor, unhappy man. He hated being born out of wedlock, he could not bear to think that, although the only son of your grandfather, he could never inherit his power and his lands. So, when your grandfather died ... when you were still but a toddler, Cecily ... he raised Galloway against me and your aunts. This was wrong of him, it could have led to war between him and the king, had he been victorious."

"But Father beat him, didn't he?" Marjory danced with relish, re-grasping her wooden weapon and slashing it through the air.

"Yes, he did," Dervorgilla laughed, standing up as Kate came bustling into the room, a page behind her carrying a rush-taper with which to kindle the wall torches.

"Oh dear, my lady. I went below to warn Bridget that last night's gruel for baby Ada was too cold, and that it must be well and truly het the night ... and that wee demon Tammy got between Bridget's legs and threw her. She cut her arm on a corner of the press ... and I'd tae stay and bind her up, ye ken."

"It's all right, Katie," Dervorgilla said. "The girls and I have had a wee chat about something; but now I must away, for I must attend to my lord's back. I'm glad you're here."

"You look tired, lassie," Kate said, gazing into Dervorgilla's face, anxious and motherly. "Must you see to the master yourself? Could yon Cedric that attends him not do it?"

"No Kate. I like to do it. And your master likes me to."

"Aye, that he does " Kate wagged her white linen-coifed head sagely

"He depends on you mair than do his babes, I'm thinking. He's graund and arrogant wi' the maist o' us but I never saw a man mair needful of his wife than him. Ye're a grand blessing to him."

Dervorgilla laughed. "Why Kate, since ever I was a bairn, I never remember such a compliment from you. Thank you."

She spoke lightly but there was a warm glow in her face. She knew her own heart was given for all eternity to Balliol. She knew that, as the years passed, he leaned more closely to her, but love? From such a one as he? In spite of assurances from her husband from time to time, she could still never quite believe that this masterful man, so much older than herself, so used to the great world of statecraft and world affairs, could truly love her, in the way she had come to adore him. Kate's words, so unusual, were like a gift.

"Goodnight lasses, ... Hugh," she added, as the boy came yawning and stretching into the room.

In the corridors and down the stone steps which ran between the children's quarters and her own, the air struck with the first hint of winter, although it was no more than late October. Dervorgilla was tired. There was always much to claim her attention even although Botel was the smallest and most homelike of all their homes. But soon she would be able to relax. She would massage her husband's scarred back and then they could sit quietly in the hall, with that new pilgrim from Jerusalem to tell them his travel-tale; there were no guests in the castle and

they could go to bed early. That would be a
luxury. Dervorgilla smiled to herself. "I think
like an old dame," she said inwardly. "Well ...
maybe I'm not so far from such a thing, after all.
I'll be coming up for forty next birthday. Many a
woman is finished by then."

In her chamber she found Balliol waiting for
her; the fire was huge, the tapestries covering the
walls were thick, there was little air and the
sconces burned quietly. John had only his
woollen shirt above his waist. As his wife came
into the room, he shouted to a page in the ante-
chamber

"Fetch the hot water and the linen. And the
salve."

"Have you been waiting long?" Dervorgilla
asked.

"Not above quarter of an hour. And I had
been glad of time to think. This matter of my
reparation to Durham ..." he grimaced with
distaste. "I must do something about it before
long. But I'm lost to know what."

Dervorgilla, finding the chamber too warm,
removed her mantle. She signalled to the page to
place the stone basin of water in its iron stand,
not too close to the fire. She waved him away.

"Shut the door and go to your meat," she
said, quietly.

She busied herself opening the lid of the salve
jar, forming a pad of the soft, worn linen. Then
she untied the strings of John's shirt and gently
eased it from his shoulders.

The scabs had long since fallen from the weals but the skin of the stripes across his back were still red. Gently she bathed his back, the water warm, soothing and sweetly scented from the dried herbs which she had sprinkled in. Rosemary was predominant. Picked from the walled herb garden on the south side of the castle. "Where rosemary grows, no poverty knows," she thought to herself, recalling a childhood rhyme picked up from dear knows where. Poverty! dear Lord ... that was one thing they certainly did not know. They were protected from much bitter misery by their wealth. Dervorgilla was thankful that she had the ease and sustenance which came from warm fires, fine clothes, dainty fare. It was not so for many souls. She thought of the poor who clustered about the castle gates each day, begging for the broken meats and stale crusts from their own tables.

She thought of Hugh, and his wish to be a scholar, a scribe ... or a minstrel. A poor, wandering minstrel. Scraps of their earlier conversation echoed in her thoughts ... A minstrel and a scholar ... a poor scholar.

"What shall I do to still that toad's croaking?" John was saying, between grunts, as Dervorgilla mopped the water from his back and began to slowly, gently, work in the salve made from almond oil, goose-grease and rose-water which, given time, would take the fire from these dreadful scars.

"I ... don't ... really ... know ..." Dervorgilla began, slowly, her words suiting her slow, rhythmical massaging.

She stopped, moved round to face her husband.

"Yes! Yes, I do know!" she exclaimed, a tide of excitement rising in her.

"John ... I should like to endow a house for poor scholars!"

"A seat of learning, eh?" the man twisted his full, red lips beneath his moustache into a half-rueful grin. "You never give up, do you? If you cannot be an Heloise yourself, then you must needs endow the Abelards of the future."

"No, but," Dervorgilla began, impatient of her husband's teasing, in love with the idea which must have lain simmering these last few months but which now burst into view so splendidly.

"There is so much to be taught; the world is just now emerging from ignorance into knowledge. We live in such an age of liberality, of open mindedness, new building, new thinking. But still the enemies lurk in the shadows ... poverty, disease, ignorance ... Oh John, let us do this. The Bishop cannot but be mollified and there is nothing finer to do with one's wealth than to show the young the way to truth ... to learning."

John looked serious. Fired by his beautiful wife's eager enthusiasm, he took her in his arms, holding her close to his breast and kissed her

with an unusual seriousness. Always, even in his
love-making, John Balliol kept the air of
detached, amused hauteur which was largely to
blame for the barrier which Dervorgilla still felt
lay, though so slightly that often she thought it
no more than her own imagination, between
them.

"Good!" he said, drawing his shirt back on.
"Good. Where shall it be sweeting? Here in
Scotland ... at Holyrood?"

"Perhaps alongside our new infirmary in
Dumfries ... the monastery is finished. The
orchards are planted on the river banks ...
the bridge itself almost finished. We could
build a small school at the top of the Friar's
Vennel?"

"But how many scholars would you find in
these rude hills?" John asked, ever practical.

"Not many, 'tis true," his wife answered,
pondering. Mayhap it would be better at
Kempston?" she raised questioning eyes to her
husband.

"Mayhap." John shook his head. He gazed at
his wife; fired with enthusiasm, her earlier pallor
had given place to a becoming bloom of colour;
in the soft light the tired lines which were
beginning to show about her eyes, had melted
away, she looked as beguiling as when he had
first wed her.

"Why not Oxford, sweetheart?" John said,
taking her hand in his own.

"Where the Franciscans and the Dominicans

... the Grey and the Black Friars have begun their teaching?"

"Yes. I have an idea that Oxford, though it be far from the city of London, may become a great seat of learning. We will endow a hostel there. My Bishop of Durham asks for a 'substantial act of charity' from me. He shall have it. I shall tell my steward at Kempston to arrange for the hire of a house. We will allow each of its inmates enough to eat, to dress themselves in simple fashion, that they may not have to toil for their bread, but can devote themselves to learning. Is that what you would like, my heart?"

"Oh, John, I should, I should," Dervorgilla answered rapturously. She took his big, brown paw and raised it to her lips. For a moment there was silence in the room save for the crackle of the fire and the spit of the sconces.

"My love," John said, gathering her to him. My serious, saintly, sweet love."

He bent his great dark head and kissed his wife with a sudden passion. As he felt her still slim, warm body against his own, her breasts pressing through his thin shirt he felt desire for her flame through him more urgently than ever before.

"The last babe was not the son I wanted," he whispered into her ear, slowly, skillfully unfastening the wimple which framed her face, loosening her still bright hair, caressing it with increasing ardour ... "but the babe we make this night shall be a son ... I know it. Heart of my life, dearest lovely one ..." his voice grew thick and blurred, he buried his lips in Dervorgilla's hair, kissed her neck, her shoulders ...

His passion lit an answering flame in her. Close they stood, close as if carved from one flesh. As one flesh, they moved from the chamber, drawn unseeing into the bedroom which lay within.

Their passionate love lay around them like an all-enveloping mantle. There was nothing in the world that cold autumn night but themselves and their love.

The world outside might say it was well-nigh winter. For them it was the high summer of their adoration for each other.

Chapter Eight

Patiently Dervorgilla repeated to her maid, Alice, her instructions about the fur robes. She wished Alice was a little quicker on the uptake, as Katie had been before she took over the nursery. On an occasion like this, with so many trunks to be packed with all the best clothes and jewellery, Katie would have done much without even being asked. Alice, though a sweet enough girl, willing and obedient, was afraid to take any initiative.

Dervorgilla sighed, then thought, repentantly, "well, she's young yet and has been with me no more than five years, when all's said and done. She will learn as she grows; experience will lend her more authority."

Aloud, she said, "Edinburgh's colder than our soft, western side ... I'll need to take my ermine cloak ... and the fox robes for the litter. Have you the key of the garde-robe? As you pass, look out to the river and see if you can see the children; they went hawking with Adam a while back; call them in, if you can."

Alice bobbed and went, on scurrying, timid feet.

Dervorgilla turned to her jewel casket. In the spring sunshine, its contents glittered and danced. What should she take for the Court visit?

She turned over the enamelled brooch set with garnets which had been part of her dower; its fine, intertwined work of Celtic design pleased her greatly. More, indeed, than the showier French jewels which her husband had given her on the birth of each child. Some of these were very fine, it was true, especially the plainer ones of warm gold but some, with their trembling diamonds and their over-busy filigree, were too elaborate for her taste.

On the other hand, to distract attention from her clumsy figure, brooches and necklets would be needed. Dervorgilla reached for a second, larger jewel-box in which were kept the biggest of her pieces. As she unlocked it's gilded lid, Marjory burst into the room, her cheeks blazing with colour, bringing the smell of fresh air underlined with a trace of horse, with her.

"Mama, Mama," she cried out, her fists clenched and her whole body tense with desire," I may come to Edinburgh with you, mayn't I?"

"No, my pet, you may not. Your father has said that Hugh and Cecily are old enough to attend the Pentecost celebrations at Court; the rest of you must wait a year or two."

"It's not fair," the child burst out ... "I know how to behave ... I would be good ..."

"Of course you would, bairnie. There, don't cry now or you'll spoil your pretty face. But you know the castle is small and there will be many of us to be housed inside its walls. We are fortunate that King Alexander was gracious enough to allow any of you young folk to go with us."

"But Cecily went with you to Whithorn last Martinmas; she goes everywhere!"

"She went to Whithorn to ask a blessing for her cough. And you, with Alex and Ada, are to go to your grand-mother at Kenmure."

"Poof ... Kenmure, I'd rathen stay here!"

"Marjory, that will do! I have much to do and have no time for tantrums. Come, help me choose my jewels for I must show what a fine lady I am, mustn't I, when I go to Court?"

Marjory recognised her mother's firmness was no longer to be tested. So, hiccuping less and less frequently, she began to paw over the beautiful ornaments in the two boxes.

"This ... you must take this," she said, laying aside a great, beaten gold breast ornament, set with amethysts and pearls. "I love this one ... and, besides, you can show everyone at Court how fine a place our Galloway is, that gives us such treasure."

"Yes," said Dervorgilla reflectively. "Amethysts from Southwick burn, pearls from our own river Dee ... and I am to wear a purple brocade gown for the feast on Sunday night. Clever Marjory," she kissed her sturdy, fiery little daughter.

"Madam," Alice broke in, her arms full of furs. "Are these the ones you wanted?"

Rising, Dervorgilla inspected the garments. "These are indeed," she said. "Did you see the children?"

"Aye, madam. Cecily and Hugh stopped to wash; they will be here soon. Madam ..." the girl seemed embarrassed.

"Madam, the garde-robe ... it stinks!" Alice was modest to a fault and this discussing of the privy, over whose window-slits furs were always hung so that the odours could keep moths off them, was painful for her. But she knew she must report truthfully to her mistress, or the health of the castle could suffer. She continued, "I think mayhap the night-soil has not been cleared for over-long from the foot of the wall below."

"Then I must speak to Rolf about it and see that it is cleaned out thoroughly. 'Tis as well we move for the summer. Otherwise we should be living on a midden; then we'd have fevers to plague us right enough."

"Yes, my lady. That's what I thought ... why I ventured to tell you."

"Pack the ermine; keep the fox blanket ready for the journey."

Cecily came into the room. She carried the same brave colour in her cheeks as her younger sister had done but painted in more delicate tones. She was growing too tall and had a willowy air about her which took the eyes of the young pages but which worried her mother.

"Is your packing finished, sweet?"

"Yes, Mamma. Everything you chose yesterday has been done; only I'm waiting for dry linen from the laundress. And I've seen my palfrey; he's no longer lame. He will walk well."

"I will ask your father to take a spare nag for you; and, if the weather be bad, as well it may be after this late frost, you shall ride in the litter with me. Marjory, take off that necklace, you will break it. Girls … away to Katie; I must be clear to think; your father wants us to start out for Dumfries at dawn tomorrow and I must be ready before dark tonight. Go now, pets."

♥ ♥ ♥

Balliol rode his black steed close to the side of the litter in which his wife travelled. They were dropping down from the hills of Galloway now, through the wooded birch glen towards the water-meadows on whose southern side the town clustered. The Queensberry hills made a fine backdrop in the clear, brisk air.

Looking down at his wife where she reclined heavily, he said,

"You do not propose to halt long at the Greyfriars' I hope?"

"Only half an hour … no more."

"Good. We must ride hard if we are to lie at Melrose. Delays are not planned for."

Dervorgilla wished her husband was sometimes in less of a hurry; he was a man with much to attend to, she conceded, but he made little allowance for the strength of others being less than his own; in her condition, she would have preferred a more leisurely journey, lying perhaps at Dumfries itself tonight instead of forcing the pace to Melrose in order to save one day. Besides, she had never yet had time to spare with her friars in their new establishment beside the Nith.

When they had crossed the fine sandstone arches of her new bridge, over the frothing water, glowing rose-red in the bright May sun, the cavalcade halted on the sandy shore of the river which ran like a girdle at the edge of the monks orchard, a colourful palette of white and pink blossom. The abbott awaited the retinue.

"I cannot tarry now," Dervorgilla said to him. "I will hope to discuss your affairs at greater length on our return from London in August or September. Only tell me now; are the bridge tolls yielding enough to support the friary?"

"Yes, my lady. But with little to spare!" The abbot was a lean man with a sense of humour like winter sun on ice; he glinted now.

Dervorgilla nodded.

Balliol interrupted.

"Abbot," he said abruptly. "Your orchard's in good flower but we are not out of the spring frosts yet; set your gardeners to light braziers among the trees and light them at dusk, tending them till the rime is off the grass each morning; do this until all danger of late frost is past or you'll lose your crop."

"Aye, my lord. Thank you. I had thought of doing so but had not yet ..."

"Come, we must away. Father, you will forgive us? We must reach Melrose before dark. If you have need, write to Rolf, my steward;

when we return at the end of summer, we will attend to your requests. Good day to you."

"God bless you, my son, my daughter ... Godspeed."

About midday the cavalcade halted at the side of a pool to refresh the horses and for the humans to eat. Hugh came up to where his mother sat in her travelling chair, the fox rug lying over her knees.

"Mother; did you ask the abbot of Greyfriars if the Book of Kells and the Book of Deer are truly being kept at Melrose just now?"

"Yes, my love. They are on loan, with other precious great volumes and parchments. You shall see them. Your great-great-grand-father, King David 1st, built Melrose Abbey and endowed it well, but since his day it has become the custom for the great abbeys to lend each other their particular treasures. You're very fortunate they should be there just now."

"I wish we could have celebrated Pentecost and the Whit feast at Melrose, instead of at the Court" Hugh said.

"Why?"

"I ... I am afraid of appearing at Court," the boy blurted out; "I should prefer to spend the feast at Melrose. I feel it is like home ... something of our very own family."

"But the Abbey of Holyrood ... that was also built by King David. Is that not then 'part of the family'?"

"It's not the same. It is too much of the smart

court world; the courtiers sneer at young country people like Cecily and me. They torment us about our clumsy shoon, our ruddy cheeks … they always have some new way of spearing their meat, of dancing and I hate all that flirting that goes on!"

"Maybe you won't find it so hard this time. After all, you are into your teens now; almost ready to be a courtier yourself. You'll see, my son," Dervorgilla laughed, "the King's court won't be so bad."

Two days later, Dervorgilla recalled the words she had spoken to her son in the wine-clear, heady air of the border hills with a pang.

The boy had been right. This was more of an ordeal than any court visit she ever remembered. The King and his consort had been kind enough, in all faith. But the court was grown corrupt as she had not remembered it before. There was a brittle air about the badinage which flew between the courtiers; their wit was spiked with malice, often as not. And the women were grown brazen in their ogling of other women's husbands, in the tightness of their bodices; more of them were painted, too, than had ever been the case before. Perhaps John was right when he said that the King was ailing more rapidly than most people realised and that, as his grasp slackened, so corruption and jealousy, position-seeking and immorality grew.

It was the Monday after Whit Sunday. The great religious festival of yester morning had

given way to a feast which was notable for its
licence. Today, there had been tourneys, jousts,
even a mock sea-battle on the Nor loch; the
common people had run races, held wrestling
bouts. Ale had been freely available all day, as
now wine seemed to be flowing without cease all
this evening.

The feast was over. The crowded hall was
filled to suffocation with the King and his court,
with barons from Normandy and England and
their ladies and aides; some were come, maybe,
like Balliol himself, to discuss with the king the
question of the succession; a delicate matter but
one that needed some attention for the young
Alexander was still but a boy. Dervorgilla knew
that already there were two factions. One, under
Durward, was for placing Scotland under feu to
England and this was the plan which Balliol
himself favoured. The other party was led by
Comyn and were all for Scotland being a
regency. Dervorgilla was torn in her own mind.
All her inclinations were to see Scotland remain
a sovereign state; yet she knew that had it not
been for the influence of the Normans and the
English, Scotland would still be a barbarian land
knowing little of good government, of law, of
husbandry, to say nothing of learning, the arts,
gentle manners. She hoped, fervently, that when
this King did die, it would not mean war ... war
between Comyn and Durward, war maybe with
England again.

The child within her stirred vigorously. If this

were the son which Balliol so dearly desired to secure his own power, he too, like Alex and Hugh, might be involved, to be slain or mangled on the battle-field. Life was very uncertain; one needed sons, so much could befall them.

"Why so pensive, sister?" The voice was mocking as ever but sharper; almost it grated upon Dervorgilla. She turned in her chair to see if it could be true ...

"Christian, I did not know you were expected! When did you come?"

"An hour or so ago." Christian's face was thinner than before, heavily painted in the new fashion; her coif was of the latest London fashion, her bosom was almost exposed beneath its weight of collars and necklaces.

"But you never come to Scotland," her elder sister protested.

"Never, if I can help it. Uncouth wilderness! But Albemarle has business with the King." Christian narrowed her eyes and said no more. Dervorgilla understood. Then it must be true. Alexander was sicker than he appeared to be. Trouble <u>was</u> brewing.

Around them the crowd was laughing now at a jester performing his sleight of hand tricks, taking liberties with his witticisms, pricking the nobles' weak points with mocking skill. The dancing bear had just finished and although most of the court and visitors conceded that it was droll enough to see the clumsy great brute gyrate, this was more to their taste.

Christian managed to squeeze onto a stool beside her sister.

"I see you are as prolific as a brood mare, yet!"

Dervorgilla blushed.

"Christian" she reproved, "Marriage is for the creation of a family."

"Some marriages may be. My old fool is impotent. And now I don't care. I would have liked babies, you know I would. But there are other things!" Her laughter was brittle.

"And how's your John these days?"

"He grows grey ... like myself. And he is too busy. 'Tis true that who has property has cares. Sometimes I long for Hugh to be grown-up so that he can take some of the burden. There is always something that must be dealt with here, in France, in London ... Northampton ..."

"They say you too, are grown quite the woman of affairs." Christian looked sharply at Dervorgilla.

"I help John where I can."

"How's your ... his penance going?"

"We are having some difficulty finding a suitable house to make into a hostel; but Rolf will look into it when we move to Fotheringhay next month; We can ride to Oxford for a few days then. We must complete the initial arrangments for my lord Bishop grows impatient and I dread another outburst from him"

"When's your babe due?"

"Next month. I plan to be in London. King Henry has sent word to John asking him to discuss funds for his fight against Gascony. Our house within the city is ready now. I shall go with John in two days' time. This will be the first child to be born in the great city of London."

Alice came behind her mistress then, tapping her arm to draw her attention.

"Cecily has a fever; her cough is back," she whispered urgently.

Dervorgilla rose. She feared for Cecily at this growing time. Alice had the medicine given her by the Cistercian Infirmarer at Dundrennan but it were better she saw for herself how her daughter fared.

"Come to my chamber in the south turret." she said to Christian. "I shall not be above half an hour; we can take a posset and talk before we sleep."

Christian for once answered gently, "I should like that."

And so, a while later, they sat, friendly enough; friendlier indeed than for many a year, Dervorgilla thought ... talking of family matters, of London fashions, of the cares of maintaining elaborate households, the unreliability of servants.

Christian yawned like a cat, stretching her thin body by the fire.

"In very truth, sister, Albemarle, and all that goes with being Albemarle's wife, weary me to desperation."

"Can you not find charity to fill your days?

There is much you could do with your wealth ... his position ..."

"I can find plenty to do with our wealth," Christian laughed, a touch of her asperity breaking into her mellower mood. "I lead fashion; my taste, my choice, in jewels, in fine furnishings ... these are acknowledged in London as the highest. That takes care of the wealth, I can assure you. Charity I leave to you, sweet sister. You have even more wealth than I, and you have the mind for staunching sores, feeding starvelings ... faugh!" She rose abruptly, striding across the room's length. She waved a hand contemptuously and was about to launch into a tirade when the door opened and Balliol came in.

He held a parchment in his hand. His expression was a mixture of jubilation and solemnity.

Without even greeting Christian or showing any surprise at finding her here in Edinburgh, he burst out,

"Your aunt Llewellyn is dead. And you are her sole heiress."

Dervorgilla's turn it was now to jump up. She took the letter from her husband's hand.

Christian whirled in a perfect fury of temper. "Her sole heiress? What of me? What of our mother? Of Helena ... her namesake even?"

"John the Scot and his wife were ever great lovers of your sister," Balliol said sternly, looking directly at his sister-in-law for the first time. You cannot put blame upon Dervorgilla that she should inherit their estates."

"Elstow ... Fotheringay ... Kempston ... Christian began to tick off on her fingers the lands which Dervorgilla now owned. "'tis monstrous!" she exploded. "I shall petition the King ... I shall make Albemarle contest the will ... Why should Dervorgilla inherit ALL? She, who has so much already. Heaven defend me, but this is more than I can bear!" Christian began to laugh and cackle hysterically ...

"Dear, sweet, pious, clever, charitable Dev," she hissed. "So good, so loyal, so loving ... yes, loving in the right quarters ... loving where it will reap her rewards ..."

"Oh, Christian ..." Dervorgilla began, unutterably distressed. "Hush, you do not mean these things. Only wait ..."

"Wait? " screamed Christian, beside herself with rage. "For what? For the man I wanted, but you took? For the babes I yearned for and you drop yearly? For the wealth which could be fashioned into art undreamed of as yet ... and which you squander on the foul-smelling serfs?"

Dervorgilla drew a deep breath; she could feel her heart fluttering.

"Christian," she said, holding out her hand to her distraught sister ... "Only let me ..."

But she had not finished the sentence when Alice came into the room, her sonsy face drained of colour ...

"Oh madam, come please. Cecily is choking;

'tis like croup; she cannot get her breath and I cannot fathom what more to do."

Dervorgilla turned and left the room behind Alice, the pair of them speeding along the dim corridor to Cecily's chamber.

♥ ♥ ♥

The crisis was over. Cecily was asleep now, breathing quietly. Dervorgilla had thrown herbs from her medicine chest, precious herbs brought from the Holy Land, upon the brazier in the girl's room, and had held her over the fumes. The vicious phlegm had been loosened. After a rubbing with medicated oil and a warm posset and instructions to Alice as to how to repeat the treatment should the attack re-occur, Dervorgilla walked wearily back towards her own room.

Why? she wondered … why was there such a feeling of doom in the air? Whitsuntide was usually the happiest season of the year; summer lay ahead, gaiety, new hope burgeoned with the young leaves. Yet already this day had seen the sad news that her beloved aunt was dead, which in turn had brought the agonising scene with Christian. Cecily, thought to be cured, was struggling for health once more. What else?

The torches in their iron holders were flickering low. The whole castle seemed to sleep. Soon she, too, could seek the release of blessed sleep, Alice she had already sent to bed. A few minutes more …

Ahead of her, in the shadows where the door

to her chamber was, on the left, Dervorgilla
suddenly saw a figure slip out of the door and
hesitate. It wore a long grey cloak. But there was
no disguising that it was a woman ...

It was Christian!

Dervorgilla's mind whirled; her tiredness
vanished in an instant. Christian? Christian
leaving the chamber where John lay? At well
nigh cock-crow?

The implication struck her like a blow. Oh no!
This monstrous thing could not be. Without
waiting to think, tormented almost beyond
sanity, Dervorgilla ran swiftly into the chamber.
John sat on the edge of the bed, his head in his
hands.

"What means this, my lord?" Dervorgilla
demanded. She stood, regally tall, a daughter of
princes indeed. Her voice cut like a rapier
through the air.

"God's blood, wife. Are you mad? Why do
you ask such a question?"

John raised his head like a bull before an
attack: His pride flared awesomely. He, too, had
had more than he could stomach. This whole
visit had been dogged by quarrels, by intrigue,
by pressuring from various of the country's
nobles who had schemes, always schemes to
further their own end. And now this!

"Don't act like a fool" he said curtly. "Come
to bed and be reasonable."

But to Dervorgilla, to whom never in her life
had any man spoken so roughly, least of all the

husband she well-nigh worshipped, his harsh words were the final blow.

She turned and left the chamber, shaking as if with ague. The great sobs began, rending her breast as if, indeed, her very heart would break.

Where could she go? Who could she turn to? She, to whom all turned for comfort, for aid ... she was alone.

With a flood of emotion uncontrollably overpowering, she knocked at the door of the tiny ante-room where Alice slept.

"Alice, Alice," she whispered urgently between sobs. "Alice ... help me. My time is come."

♥ ♥ ♥

The boy who was born as the grey, wet dawn broke, lived only long enough to be christened by the castle's priest. Alan, they called him. Alan of Galloway, he would have been, had he lived. Alan of Galloway, like his grandfather before him.

Balliol only saw the son he'd so greatly desired for one, anguished moment, as he lay, shrouded and so dreadfully still. This was to have been the son who would ensure the name of Balliol against all disaster. This was the baby to have been born in the gay heart of the great city of London. This was the boy who, if all went as Balliol dreamt, could have been, given a twist or two of Fate's wheel, King of Scotland himself.

Now, he was nothing but a scrap of flesh, lifeless, hopeless.

And between the man and the woman who had created him with such passion, such consuming love, each for the other, lay a gulf equally lifeless and hopeless.

Balliol wept for more than his son.

Chapter Nine

"Quick, put the ink-stand on it's corner 'ere it blows away," Balliol said, placing his great hand on a corner of the parchment as the frolic breeze blew in from the open casement.

The slim young man with the anxious face, moved the pewter ink-holder to one corner of the drawing and Dervorgilla secured a third with the key of her writing chest, wrought iron and heavy enough to defy any summer wind.

Through the window the first heat of an early June wafted; the noise of the London street below came with it, as did the stench of the gutters and a pair of flies. She thought of her Galloway hills and how soon she could return to enjoy their peace.

"Madam," Balliol's voice brought her back from her daydreams. It was not harsh but there was a colder note in it than ever before. This past year had not healed the agonizing rift between them.

"Master Alfred must to Fotheringhay today. Let us be done with this business as speedily as we can."

Dervorgilla turned her attention to the drawing before her. "I approve of Master Alfred's design," she said quietly. "'I have nothing to add. I think it will be an improvement." she said. "Fotheringhay's main hall is a gey draughty place; if Master Alfred can make it snugger, that's all I ask."

"Well, if you approve it, that's good enough. You've a better eye for these things in plan than I have. I prefer to make my judgment as the building rises on the spot. I'm no theorist," Balliol said, stretching. "Action's my meat. Though with all this business of the new young king of Scotland, I've had more than my fill of action; I know that road north like I know the way to my bed. And now this business in Vimeu … I'll needs must cross to France by the next boat."

He stared out of the window to where a glimpse could be seen of the Tower of London.

"My kinsman of Picardy may have had a genius for building, and for building stout," he added, almost to himself. "I confess I feel at a loss when I see these," he waved a hand at the young man's drawings for the improvements to Fotheringhay. "These scribblings. 'Tis you, my dear, who are the builder."

"When you have attended to this matter," Dervorgilla said to the young architect, "will you draw me plans for a priory? A small one. I have it in mind to give something of the sort to Wigtown, not far from where St. Ninian's chapel lies. It's wild, barbarous country and the people need the teachings which the monks of such an establishment could give."

"Happily, madam," the architect replied, rolling up his precious parchment and taking his leave.

There was silence in the room after he had left; not an unkind silence, yet neither was it a friendly one.

"John," Dervorgilla began, finally. "Whilst we speak of building, I would ask your indulgence to consider something which is growing in my mind, growing very dear to it."

John turned without speaking and looked at his wife seriously, a trifle sadly, maybe but with an underlying coolness as if he were weighing her up.

"I have a notion to build an Abbey," she began, slowly. "There is a place, beside the burn at the eastern end of Criffel, in a small plain not far from the Solway shore, which breathes peace. There, I would fain endow ..."

She was interrupted by a knock at the door. Rolf the senechal, burst in excitedly, travel-stained, his riding gloves swishing in his strong, brown hands. There was a burst from below as of a street brawl. Balliol drew the casement close irritably and turned to his steward.

"I've found a house ..." Rolf began. "The right place ... the right price ... for the poor scholars." His hazel eyes glowed with pleasure.

"How much?"" Balliol asked.

"I cannot find a place to buy, sire," Rolf answered, "but this is a sizeable house for hire not far from the centre of the village. 'Twould make a suitable alms-house."

"How many scholars could it house?" Dervorgilla asked.

"About fifteen, madam."

" 'Tis small," Dervorgilla said, thoughtfully plucking her lower lip.

"Big enough," her husband growled. " 'fore God, madam, you'll ruin us with your passion for building and endowing." His tone was not entirely serious but Dervorgilla, still ultra sensitive about this man who had hurt her so greatly, fell silent.

"How much?" he asked again.

"The hire is but twenty pounds per year. To keep, say, fifteen poor boys, to provide teachers, books, fire, food for them ... mayhap some £40 pounds more each year."

Balliol turned to his wife.

"What say you, my lady? Can we afford this sum, for ever and all eternity?"

"Yes, John, I think so." Dervorgilla raised her eyes to look her husband squarely in the face. Her heart gave a sudden pain as she did so. She loved this burly man with the greying hair and beard, so dearly. Why had he betrayed her and shattered their life so utterly?

"I will consult with our accounts," she continued, "while you are in Picardy; but I am very sure we can arrange for this thing. It will appease my lord bishop for all time, and ... it will please God, I think," she added, simply.

"Learning is the key to all ills. If we can but sweep aside the ignorance which breeds poverty, disease and hatred between people, then we shall have made the world more to God's liking."

"See to it then," Balliol ordered Rolf. "Get the papers drawn up. When I return from France I must to Scotland again to forestall Comyn. I will be at Botel by the time of the harvest, I think. Come to me then, Rolf and I will sign."

"Shall I scout out a likely tutor, sire, and attend to the making of the desks, the beds, the hiring of cooks and cleaners?"

"Aye," said Balliol. "But commit me to nothing until you see me at Botel. And Rolf ... hire no pretty maids. Young scholars must not be distracted from their books!" A flash of white teeth between sensual lips. Rolf grinned happily at his master and left.

Dervorgilla rose from her seat before the great oaken table where the plans of Fotheringhay's new hall had been spread, and sat down beside the empty fireplace, filled now with summer lupins. She took up her embroidery frame and began to stitch.

"John," she said, "what meant you ... that you must forestall Comyn?"

"Comyn is burning to form a Scottish Nationalist party," he said. "He would put us back two centuries, cutting us off into an inward-looking parish-pump state, undoing all that has been achieved since King William's 'Auld

Alliance' which first brought enlightenment to Scotland."

"But can you trust Durward?" Dervorgilla asked.

"Not entirely. Black Douglas thinks Durward has designs upon the throne of Scotland for himself. I don't agree. But I do think he will put, perhaps, too much influence on the young Alexander if he can. English Henry fears this too, I know. But not so much as he fears Comyn and the Nationalists."

"What can you do, John, as a Regent of Scotland to prevent bloodshed, maybe even civil war in Scotland?"

"I can supply English Henry with money, that's one thing. And so long as he remains in my debt, he will have to suppress Comyn's faction." He turned from pacing the room. "You see, my dear, why I cannot whole-heartedly entertain your schemes for monkish building. There are other things to be done with wealth. Wealth is a tool and a mighty sharp one. One can never have too much power and power stems from property."

Dervorgilla remained silent. This was an aspect of John which she disliked ... and feared. In the days before little Alan's death, she would have spoken softly about the spiritual matters which she believed were more important than earthly affairs. Now, she felt too estranged from Balliol to embark on such a discussion.

She was spared from continuing their brink-poised conversation by a further arrival. This one was totally unexpected. So unexpected, in fact, that Dervorgilla rose to her feet in alarm, a sense of foreboding sweeping through her. Balliol, too, startled by their unaccustomed visitor, moved closer to his wife, and laid a comforting hand upon her brocade sleeve.

The stringy, bent man who came in was none other than William de Fortibus, Christian's despised husband. For no other reason than that he disliked most people and was indifferent to everything other than his own poor health, de Fortibus had never been close to his wife's family. He did not bear them the rancour which she had borne, but then he felt nothing stronger than a flutter of fear when his breath came shorter than usual at any time in his life. He neither liked nor disliked the great Balliol and his beautiful wife. He had a sufficiency of wealth himself to sustain him in his quiet immolation; the world of fashion, the world of politics, of sport, of battle ... none of these were for him. His life consisted of forever experimenting with the new pills and potions which his physician concocted for him, with examining and recording his various ills and afflictions. His pleasure came from studying old manuscripts which various agents up and down the land unearthed for him. Some said he was a sorcerer. In fact, he was as ineffectual and unremarkable as a fly, left over from summer, hanging around the kitchen in winter's unaccustomed air.

He stood now, leaning on his stick, his wispy ginger hair, fading into an unpleasing yellow, sticking unbecomingly from beneath his cap. His breathing was hard as if he had hurried and his red-rimmed eyes looked rheumier than usual.

"Greetings," he said, in a muffled voice.

Balliol recovered from his surprise sufficiently to drag forward a chair and to assist de Fortibus to its support

"I bring you ill news."

"Christian?" Dervorgilla asked, aware of something unpleasant.

"She died last night."

"Died?" Dervorgilla echoed. "But, she was only forty-one ... no, forty-two ... What was it? Plague?"

Her mind leapt back to the last time she'd seen her sister, a year ago. Her face had been thin, it is true, and perhaps too highly coloured; but hadn't that been rouge? And, in the oasis of time when they'd discoursed so pleasantly, as sisters might be expected to do, she had made no mention of any ailment.

"She had a canker within; it could not be stopped. It ate out her very being." de Fortibus sniffed and searched for a handkerchief with which to clear the tears.

"She did not tell me." Dervorgilla said, beginning to cry in her turn.

"She told no-one, save, latterly, myself."

"Poor, poor girl. Chris ... oh my poor Chris," Dervorgilla whispered.

"Aye, poor Christian indeed. She was a tormented soul," the widower said.

"In these last months 'twas as if she were eaten not only by the canker within her bowels, but by a very fox of madness at times. She would stay awake all night long, drawing, drawing ... jewels, furniture; she had dreams ... fevers you could call them ... she would order box after box of colours; her crayons and pencils were never right. She terrorised her ladies in waiting. Then, there would come calm spells when she would be sweet as I have never known her, in all our life together. She would sit, quiet, at a window, maybe her hand on her chin, gazing at nothing, saying nothing." The man broke down again "I did not understand her," he said, after a quiet spell, with a simple honesty which brought fresh tears to Dervorgilla's eyes.

Balliol all the while stood like a rock, saying nothing.

"She had strange whims. She could not be denied. Once she brought all the village children into the house. She bade the servants make up beds for them all with our best linen sheets. She bathed them, with the help of her tiring woman, she arrayed them in the finest clothes she could lay hands on, ripping off the hems of her gowns in order to make them fit, pinning the brats into folds that well nigh stifled them." de Fortibus paused, sighed for his own martyrdom and continued. "I could not stop her. No-one could stop her. She fed those village blockheads with every delicacy she could think of, even wine, until they vomited at table. Then she grew furious and bid her maids bundle them out into the night. She would not speak to me for days thereafter. I did not understand her."

Dervorgilla did. And what she understood caused her to grieve even more for this strange, unhappy creature whom, all her life, she had never managed to reach, to help, or to succour.

"Aye," de Fortibus went on, sniffing, "She was neither to hold nor to bind. One night, here in London, she opened her dining room window ... we were alone that evening ... and flung out some of her silver-gilt plate to the passers-by. I could not recover it," he added, with a sudden swing to self-interest and the cautious habits of a lifetime.

"Strangest of all," he added, looking up, forgetting to weep in the wonder of his news, "To you, madam, she has left her entire fortune." As Dervorgilla gasped and gaped at him, he hurriedly added, "Not that it is an overwhelming amount I must tell you, she was too extravagant for that, although I did what I could to husband her inheritances."

"Me? I am heiress to Christian's wealth?"

"Who else? I thought she ... she ... hated ... disliked you. But Helena is gone, your mother too ... I do not need ... Who else?"

"Aye." For the first time Balliol broke into the conversation, "Had she not willed it, the King would have seized it, true enough. But t'were more fitting it should have gone to you, de Fortibus."

"Perhaps so," the old man wheezed. "Perhaps so. But I do not need it." He rose, leaning heavily on his jewelled cane. "Besides ... she could not be stalled from doing other than this. She would not tell me why. Two days ago, she made the will. When she knew her end was not far away. 'Dev will understand,' she said."

At this, Dervorgilla was torn with grief. She did not understand this strange, last act of her tormented sister. But she could understand that she must have died as unhappily as she had lived.

William de Fortibus was taking his leave of them now, He could not bear the sight of Dervorgilla's grief; his own was sufficient.

As he left, he murmured to Balliol about "law clerks, probate, papers."

Dervorgilla was choked with sobs. As Balliol turned from the door, closing it quietly, he crossed the room and took his wife in his arms. Cradling her as he would have done one of the children in distress, he hushed her grief, speaking no word, only holding her close, rocking her gently to and fro. Presently he drew her down to sit beside him on a cushioned settle, still holding her hands.

"I do not understand," Dervorgilla said at last, when her sobs had grown quiet.

"Nor do I ... not entirely," John said.

"I feel as if ... as if she were accusing me from the grave ... as if she were saying 'see what I can give you; you who gave me nothing'."

"Mayhap she is. Mayhap it is some kind of retribution she seeks from the grave. Or," the big man continued, gently massaging her white hands with his thumbs, "Maybe she thought of this as some kind of ..." he almost said "payment", but sought for a better word ... "amend," he finished lamely.

"But she knew I had more than enough money; that I do not like wealth and the burdens it brings."

"Then perhaps she left you her gold to spite and hurt you, even from the grave," John said, he spoke with vigour "She was a bitch, possessed of an evil heart and mind." he spoke with cutting bitterness and rancour.

"John!" Dervorgilla was shocked to the marrow of her being. "Do not speak like that. Your soul will burn in hell to talk so of the newly dead." She made the sign of the cross on her bosom.

"I don't think so," her husband replied stoically. "A just God, and he is just, although we cannot always see it so, would never punish a mortal merely for speaking the truth."

Dervorgilla was silent. Her heart pounded, her cheeks were beginning to take on a staining of high colour. She knew that a vital moment had arrived in her life. It must be now that she summon up her courage, if she were to save her marriage and bring it back to warm life, as it had been until a year ago. Inwardly she prayed to be able to find the right words.

"Was she wicked ... or just sick ... my sister?"

"Both."

"How do you know?"'

"From the first time I ever set eyes on her, she desired me, as wantonly as any tavern strumpet."

Dervorgilla made an involuntary gesture of distaste.

"Nay, sweet," John said, quietly. "I did not blame her. 'Twas a fire in the blood which she could not quench; some women are like that."

Dervorgilla caught at the endearment which had slipped out so naturally and her heart began to sing even while she told herself that it was nothing, merely long use and the carelessness wrought by absorption in so serious a matter.

"She could not be blamed for something she could not help. 'Tis no more than being born with black hair or gold. But she allowed it to grow and to take hold of her, instead of trying to tame it. I never understood why your mother, or your father for that matter, did not try to rein her in."

"My mother did, I think," said Dervorgilla, thoughtfully. "But Chris was ever high spirited and quarrelsome. And she and my mother grated upon each other like tinder and flint. I think my mother felt, as Chris grew into womanhood, it was better not to stir the dislike which lay between them."

"And then," Balliol went on, "to marry such a lass to an old maid like Fortibus!"

"My father arranged that for political reasons."

"As he did our own marriage?" Balliol looked at his wife with softer eyes than at any time during the past twelve months. Her cheeks crimsoned now almost painfully. She bent her head and withdrew her hands from his gentle clasp.

"But …," she began presently, a little breathless. "You said that Chris was sick, too?" She paused, delicately. "How do you know … I mean, before this afternoon?"

Balliol put a hand under his wife's chin and raised her face where the colour still glowed. He gazed into her deep green eyes.

"Because she told me so. On that night."

Dervorgilla looked startled, Balliol nodded slowly, dropped his fingers to interlace them once more with his wife's.

"That night, after you'd gone to Cecily, I calmed her down and she left my room." For a moment a quizzical smile lay about the man's lips as he recalled the events of that spring night. "She didn't want to go … not she. But I made her. Then," he continued, looking again into Dervorgilla's anxious eyes, "she returned. Quite some time later I heard a noise at the door. I thought it was you, so I awoke and opened the door. Christian stood there. She was distraught. My first instinct was to shut her out. But she pushed wildly into the room, weeping as if her very soul was damned. She was clawing at her belly and I could see, even before she told me, that she was in great pain. I fetched some

laudenum from my travelling medicine box in
the ante-room and made her take a little. She
began to calm down, and it was then she told me
what she knew ... had known for long enough.
That she harboured a canker in her guts which
the physicians declared would kill her within
twelve months."

"Oh," Dervorgilla breathed. "Poor, poor
Chris," she murmured, the tears springing anew
to her eyes.

"Aye, poor Chris. God give her soul peace."

"And that ... that was ... all?"

"Yes."

For a long moment, while a stray pigeon
cooed at the window in the grey dusk which was
dimming the gold of the day, there was no word
spoken in the small chamber. Then Dervorgilla
slipped to her knees and burying her head in her
husband's hands, murmured,

"Oh forgive me, forgive me."

The burly shoulders bent over the frailer form.

"My heart, gladly."

His lovely wife raised her tear-stained face.
"All these months I have been blaming you for
hurting me," she said, fixing him with her great
eyes. "But it is I who hurt you." She looked for
words but none other would come.

"Sweeting," John said, raising her to her feet
and standing with her against his heart, looking
steadily at her. "We have hurt each other, but
God willing, we shall not do so again. We must
not do so again. I grow old, my sweeting."

Dervorgilla made a little noise of protest.

"Oh yes, I do." John laughed, kissing the tip of her nose lightly.

"Even you," he said, playing with a strand of hair which had escaped the jewelled net which bound his wife's heavy tresses, "sport a little grey now, where all was gold before." He grew suddenly serious, straining Dervorgilla close, close to him.

"We have no time to waste in hurt. We are much blessed that love lives between us. Let us cherish from now until ..." He stopped speaking to close their two mouths with a deep, passionate kiss.

Chapter Ten

"Such a snow-storm in March." Katie fumed as a fresh flurry of hail jostled against the windows of the bed chamber where she bustled about with a small tub of water before a leaping fire.

"But we often get such a storm at winter's end." Dervorgilla said softly, from the silk pillows where, propped up, her hair streaming around her, she sat nursing her newest babe. "But, I like it," she went on dreamily, cuddling the small scrap in swaddling clothes to her, watching his crumpled face as he lay in sleep. "It is good to lie cosily in a clean bed, warm, safe, content. Life is very good, Kate."

"Aye, ma doo it is. When it is!" Kate groaned a little as she shook some rosemary into the steaming water and bent her back to swirl the herb into its depths. "But if you're as creaky as ah'm growing, it's no jist such a bed o' roses as it might be for some of us."

"Oh, Kate, is it bad again, the pain?" her mistress responded with quick sympathy.

"Bad eneuch. But then, what can you expect, in a cauld rife spot like Gallowa'? I'm lucky I'm not screws from head to toe."

"Kate, when I'm up and about again, I'll send for that Saracen healer. My lord tells me he does wonders for his back with his supple fingers and his unguents."

"Deed you'll no!" Kate shrilled. "I'm having no heathen body at me. Na, na. My auld faither was crippled near like a shepherd's crook afore he went to his Maker and same'll be my lot; but it's the lot of the maist o' us hereabouts and I'll just accept it as the wull o' God. Here you, Ben," she broke off, stirring a collie pup with a guardian foot. "Oot o' that ye heathen." She winged an elbow towards the dog who moved swiftly away from the tub where he'd been sniffing, to sprawl nearer to the log's heat.

Dervorgilla laughed. It was a happy sound, like a young burn gurgling through the heather.

"Aye, Katie dear. We all grow older. But, thank heaven," she whispered, gazing at her baby, "I'm not too old yet." A secret small smile flickered about her lips and she sighed from pure happiness.

"Ye're right happy, mem, aren't ye?" Katie said, more gently than usual, as she moved towards the bed to take the infant from his mother.

"Aye, Kate, I am. Happier now than ever in my life before," her mistress answered as she slipped out of the bed and sat down on a bench before the tub, where she began to strip off her night-robe.

"Wait now, wait a bittie," the old nurse said. "You're just a week delivered. Dinna be tottering into the fire. Wait till I put the wee mannie into his cradle and I'll be there directly to gie ye a haun'."

"I can manage," said Dervorgilla, slipping into the warm water. "Oh, but it's good to be safely delivered of that boy," she said, revelling in the caress of the warm, scented bath.

"Aye, that it is. He's a fine lusty lad too. He'll do well for his faither before he's finished."

"It's good to have him especially now that Hugh's away on the Crusade and Alexander's troubled with his chest. What is it, Kate, that ails my children?"

"Well, lassie, I don't know that you could say anything rightly ails them. It's the usual thing for bairns to have hoasts. And that was all i' truth, that Cecily had, or that wee Alex has now. We're all due our bit ills o' the flesh, ye ken. The good Lord said we were and he was right."

"Kate, Kate....dear Kate....you're as staunch as Bengairn," Dervorgilla laughed. "Hand me my fresh gown, will you?"

"Well, we'll just towel your ladyship first," Kate said, enveloping her mistress in a great sheet of rough linen. "Aye, ye're no a bad shape even yet. Fer yer age, ye're gey jimp."

"I'll need tight binding for a while, though," Dervorgilla replied lightly. "I've little waist left. Seven bairns don't exactly help to keep one lissome as a lassie!"

"Weel and a'," Kate conceded, "Ye're no sae bad, all thing's considered. Sit there now, ma doo, and I'll brush your hair."

Kate brushed quietly for a moment or two, crooning an old cradle song, The baby snuffled a little in his sleep; Ben twitched, catching rabbits in his sleep, his paws working as if he were running over the moor; a log burnt through and fell with a small thunder into the hearth. Dervorgilla sat, wrapped in her happiness as if in a mantle of softest down. She did not hear the door open, softly.

Nor, for a long moment or two did she know that the brushing upon her hair had subtly altered. Then she became aware of firmer stroke. She half turned, but before she could quite do so, she felt a man's strong hands go over her eyes.

"John?" she said, happily.

"No other." He kissed her brow, then slipped round to seat himself beside her on the bench. Kate had crept away. They were alone save for the infant in his cradle in the shadowy corner of the great chamber. The storm was blowing itself out now, its gusts less vicious, its icy fingers less tempestuous in their snatchings at the old castle.

"I've just finished conferring with Durward," Balliol said, unloosening his surcoat before the fire's heat. "Now, I can spend time to dally with my sweetheart." He pressed his wife to his heart, kissing her lightly on the eyes.

"God's shoon, sweet, you never looked lovelier! We must make more babies. It suits you!" He laughed joyously.

"Hush, John. You'll wake the babe."

"What of it? I like to see my son's eyes ... he's the only one yet to look like you."

"Ah, but he'll change."

"So long as he stays like you, heart's love, he'll do well."

Dervorgilla was suddenly serious.

"I think he will do well, John. There is something ...something very special about this child."

"There is indeed." This time John kissed his wife full on her lips.

"I don't mean that. But I feel a kind of destiny about this boy. As if some high fate will be his."

"All Balliols have a high fate." John said with mock arrogance, puffing up his chest.

Dervorgilla dissolved into laughter, sheltering in the strength of her husband's shoulder.

"Time will tell, my love," she said.

"Speaking of time, I must leave you soon."

"Already? Oh no."

"I fear this Regency for young king Alexander is going to cause trouble; I must to Edinburgh to speak to Durward."

Far away, behind the last sullen rattle of hail, an animal howl echoed in the forest. Dervorgilla shivered.

"Sounds like a wolf," she said.

"Aye, there's a few of the brutes living yet."

Dervorgilla twisted herself free from her husband's encircling arm.

"John," she said, her face serious. "Before you go, I want to ask your advice. That money of

Christian's has troubled me, as you know, I've sought about for some good work to use it on. Now, young Mattie, Kate's under-nursemaid, comes from north of Edinburgh, at yon wee town of Dundee and she tells me there's a mighty need of teaching and of nursing. I have grown greatly to fancy creating a Friary....or a monastic foundation of some kind, What do you think?"

John gazed at his lovely wife's face, so earnest, so dearly beloved with the passing years. Although he enjoyed the homage and gratitude which came to him as a result of carrying out those acts of charity which befitted his high estate, his heart was not much moved by this side of his activities as one of Britain's greatest barons.

Getting up, pulling his surcoat straight, easing his undergarments into more comfortable positions, he smiled indulgently, He bent to kiss his wife's nose; "Sweetheart, I think it's an excellent idea. Speak to Rolf about it ... see if you can find a suitable site. It's to be for the Cistercians, I suppose?"

Dervorgilla nodded, a small smile admitting her fondness for this particular order.

"When I return from Edinburgh, we'll make firm plans. Now go I must."

There came another rattle of wind and rain at the window.

"I wish you'd not to ride north on such a night," Dervorgilla whispered, unwilling for the tranquil mood to be broken.

"I like it not, myself. Sometimes I think there's too much silver in my pow these days for such scuttlings up and down the length of the land. Next thing will be a summons to help English Henry out of his French troubles! And Rolf tells me there have been some skirmishes around our boundaries with Annandale's rogues. They've lain quiet this many a year. But I suppose we were bound to have trouble with them again, the Bruces and the Balliols were old enemies in France, my father used to say, long before they ever set foot in Galloway."

"I didn't know that," Dervorgilla said, watching her husband stretch his legs about the chamber, flexing his muscles, subconsiously preparing himself for his cold ride through the night.

"Aye, the two families were at one time ... some generations back mark you, neighbours and right good quarrelers, it seems! There seems to have been a good seed of jealousy sown somewhere."

"Oh John, I hope we can remain at peace. Somehow, since wee John's birth I have felt that our worst troubles were by, that we'd reached a kind of plateau, a safe level in our life: I wish it would be so. We've seen enough of storm ..."
She was interrupted by a rattle of the door-latch.

Kate came bursting into the room evidently greatly agitated. "Oh, madam," she burst out, even as, catching sight of Balliol, she sketched a curtsey to him. He turned, severe-eyed, frowning at her unceremonious entry.

"Mem," Kate continued, unable to withold her tale, be her lord as vexed as thunder. "It's young Cecily, She's eloped with Master Giles, your lordship's new young squire."

Balliol let out a bellow fit for a bull.

"God's night-shirt," he roared, "She's but a bairn! What in all the saints' names were you thinking of, woman, to let such a thing happen?" he glowered at the nurse until, as she said in awe to Mattie later, he could have gored and trampled her to death on the spot, bull-like in very truth.

"Dervorgilla, you must have been lax with your daughter," he continued. Then, impatient, as if stung by wasps, he shook his head, sketching an abrupt motion with his hand. "Dear God, we're but wasting time here.

"Run, Kate ... alert the guard, find Rolf ... I'll ride after them and stop them."

"They'll have gone Kirkcudbright way, sire," Kate bustled around her master while Dervorgilla, still weak from child-birth, tried ineffectually to rise, although what she was about to do she could not have told.

"How do you know of this, Kate?" she asked in low, fearful tones.

"Wee Mattie found a note pinned to Cecily's pillow when she went to bed the young ones and to prepare Cecily's chamber for the night. I've thought for a while that there was a bit of sheep's eyes gaein' on ..."

"Stop your chatter female. Get down to the guard, tell the stables I'll need my best horse, my fastest one ... hurry!"

Dervorgilla looked so pale, so distraught, "Where's my 'plateau of safety' now?" she murmured, twisting her hands together, "Oh John, find her; she's just a baby ..."

"She's nigh seventeen," Balliol growled. "Old enough to feel the stirrings in her loins... she's more like me than you, my dear, who slept innocent for over-long in your own youth. But I'm to be off. God knows when I'll return. But don't worry. If I find this idiot pair I'll despatch them straight home with some of my men and continue for Edinburgh. Don't fret, my sweet."

"God speed, John," Dervorgilla said, half-raising herself from her seat, to receive her husband's hasty kiss.

He went out, leaving the door unlatched so that a bitter draught sneaked in, causing the wall sconces to flutter and the fire to puff smoke into the room, The baby in the cradle cried. His mother turned her head towards him; her thoughts were sad. These children! Born in love, or in mere resignation, in hatred, always in pain; what lay before them? Cecily! Such a child, and running off like this. She, who'd always seemed such a douce wee maid. If Cecily could cause such anguish, what of pert Marjory almost her equal in age and more than her equal in mischief always.

Maybe there was never any 'plateau' in life;

nothing but everlasting problems, strife, challenges. Dervorgilla found her legs trembling, like a birch leaf in a spring breeze, and in the small of her back a gnawing pain began to thrust itself into her attention, throb, throbbing, Time she returned to her bed. As she uncertainly began to move away from her seat before the fire, the chamber door was pushed open once again; this time it was a timid Mattie who came in, her face scarlet at having to speak directly to her lady, without the protective bulwark of Kate between herself and the grandness of the Lady Dervorgilla.

Stuttering, Mattie said, "My ladyship … yon bairn,…I mean, wee Ada … oh, yer ladyship … Madam …" she paused, twisting her pudgy fingers together in an agony of apprehension, although her mistress was looking at her with kindly eyes.

"Go on, lassie. What is it that troubles you? What's wrong with Ada?"

"Nocht much … but I canna sort it masel' … it's … it's her chamberpot, mem … it's stuck!"

"Slowly, Mattie. What are you trying to tell me?"

"That wee lamb o' … " Mattie was almost beside herself now, partly with embarrasment at what she had to say added to her natural shyness when speaking to her ladyship, and partly because she felt that she had betrayed her duty to her charge in allowing this contretemps to take place at all.

"Mattie," Dervorgilla broke in, "please, I must know ... is anything really wrong with Ada?"

"Not all that wrong, mem ... but no' awfy right, ayther," she burst out.

"She's gone and got her head stuck into her night chamber pot!" she finally blurted the words out. "There was sic a stir aboot the place with Katie running demented-like; I took ma een off her, Ada I mean, mem, for but a wee minute. An' I canna loose her, try how I will, And she's greetin' sair. Can ye come, mem?"

Dervorgilla astonished the serving girl by sitting down on the settle and bursting into laughter. With more than a touch of hysteria, she laughed and laughed. After all the emotions of this evening ... her early rapture, her anxiety over Cecily's running-off ... now this domestic chaos!

Mopping her eyes, Dervorgilla fought for self-control. She met Mattie's bewildered expression with a smile.

"I can't manage to come myself," she said. "But if you will carry Ada to me and fetch ..." she thought for a moment. Rolf, her invariable mainstay, was away with John. "Yes ... ask one of the pages to fetch the blacksmith. I will try to soothe the lassie until he comes; he can cut the pewter no doubt, with his great pliers, and we'll free the poor bairn! Run, Mattie and let us have an end to the ploys of this night."

Chapter Eleven

"I love autumn," Dervorgilla said. "Especially here at Botel, where I can smell the salt of the sea coming on the wind from Rough Firth, and see the purple of the heather fading from my hills." She sewed calmly at her tapestry.

John, sitting on the stone bench beside her, answered. "Aye," he said, raising his eyes to the mellow blue and gold of the day, warmer than usual for October. "It's a goodly place, our Botel. I'll confess that when I first saw Alan of Galloway's domain I thought it a brutish, untamed place. Yet I'm never more at ease than here."

He laid his brown hand, on whose wrist the hairs were white now, on his wife's thigh, "You've made me a happy man, my love," he said, stooping towards her to kiss her cheek. "You're a bonny lass even yet."

"Oh John," Dervorgilla laughed, "only in your eyes." She looked at him with adoration and her heart skipped a beat, as it had done when she was still a young bride. "I'm afraid that to younger folk I'm nought but a hag. Young John, this very morning, told me that I was too old to understand his troubles!"

With a return to his old fire, Balliol growled

"And what are that young popinjay's troubles as of this moment? Is he making trouble again? I'll put him into squire service with de Quincy, as I threatened to do before, if I have much more of his nonsense!"

"Ssh ... 'tis only a lad's wilfulness, he's heard talk of this de Montfort and his new ideas that the barons should be stripped of their power and he says he wants to join his party; and why dont we go south now instead of waiting for Michaelmas?"

Balliol turned to look in amazement at his wife. His hair and his eyebrows were white, his face deep furrowed and marked with the years; but his brown eyes shone with fire still.

"He's scarce into his teens and he speaks thus?"

"There are many new ideas abroad, John," Dervorgilla said deprecatingly laying her needlework in her lavender-silk lap. "Ideas fly through the air very easily these days since men have bred faster horses and roads spread across the world like new veins every other year. You cannot halt progress."

"Progress? Progress? You call it progress when insolent cubs turn against their fathers? Madam, I thought you'd more sense!" He softened for a moment, "But you'd ever liberal ideas; what was it you used to say about preferring to be a poor scholar than a rich baron's wife? But it's rubbish, my dearling, rubbish. There must always be those who rule the unlettered, and who, in doing so, amass wealth. It's the way of the world. He'll learn better with the years. Is he not interested in his own inheritance, by God?"

"No doubt. Our John loves gold well enough and all the finery it can buy. But ..." Dervorgilla paused. "I think he feels that as the younger son he cannot hope for more than his due share of what we shall leave."

"There are only the two boys since Alex met his death fighting the infidel. Can he not find himself sufficiently well-dowered? God's shoon, these children of ours are heirs to one of the largest fortunes in all Europe. And yet he would deprive us ... and himself ... of our wealth? The boy's an idiot ... worse, he's a traitor to his own. Where is he? I'll attend to him."

"He's gone hawking with Ada. For all she's a matron now of some six months' standing, she loves to ride over the moors."

"As do I, my heart, she's like me. Truth to tell, I weary now of statecraft, of kings and politics. But I love three things as much as ever I did. You ... Botel ... and riding free."

Dervorgilla had resumed her embroidery. She looked slyly at her husband.

"Your ale no longer, my lord?"

He let out a great belly laugh. "Aye, I still love my ale. And my meat, thank God. I was blessed with strength and a healthy carcase. I'll die active, I think!"

Like a cloud-shadow over the silken autumn

sea, a change of mood darkened Dervorgilla's serenity.

"John, I want to speak to you about that."

He refused to be serious. "My death? Woulds't be a wealthy widow so soon?"

She only shook her head, used to his teasing, refusing to look in the face the inescapable truth, that, being almost twenty years older than herself, this beloved husband of hers must, in the nature of things, leave her to spend the last portion of her life alone.

"You know that for long now I've thought to build a resting place for our mortal remains? We've done much, you and I, for the brothers of St. Francis; now, it comes strongly upon me that I should dearly love to copy my ancestor King David who brought that other order, the monks of Cisterce to the valleys of Melrose and of Dundrennan."

"Tillers of soil? Do you think that would be a suitable resting place for my bones? A quiet valley encircled with sheep on the hill, footed by peaceful fishers?"

"My heart, you have the wrong idea of the Cistercians. I am drawn to them because they, like you, are hard men, men who have cast off luxury and soft living; they are men of action ..."

With a gleam of amused malice, John interrupted, "Rather than men of wisdom and learning?"

Dervorgilla had no time to reply before a youth of not more than fifteen raced down the flagged path between the rich mosaic of the autumn flower beds alive still with the golds, the tawnies, the purples and smoke-blues of their late flowers.

"Father," he cried, in a voice between that of a boy and a man, "a messenger's just ridden in. It seems Uncle de Quincy is dead, Does that mean you will take over the lordship of Western Galloway too, now?"

The old man rose to his feet. In a quiet, level tone, under-towed with sarcasm, he surveyed this, his youngest and last child, with cool eyes.

"No, boy, it does not. Your uncle's affairs will be taken care of ... and right ably, I'm misdoubting ... by his son-in-law, young Comyn, and his two brothers-in-law."

The boy's face assumed a sulky expression.

"But the Comyns are a plundering lot," he burst out.

"What do you know about it?"

"I know this much, John Comyn of Badenoch is called 'The Wolf' and rightly so, on account of his plundering and ..."

"Don't be a fool, my son" Balliol said.

Dervorgilla saw the red flare in her husband's cheeks. She dreaded lest his fire should burst against his son. Life was so strange. Balliol as much as herself...more so...had desired this last son to secure his inheritance. Yet, of all their children, this boy irritated and troubled his father as none other had done. They were like oil and water, like sea and rock; one fretted the other continually and could not mingle happily. She must speak to Abbess Beatrice when next they visited Kempston; she was wise in the ways of young folk. Perhaps she could offer some counsel.

"The air grows cool. I think I will retire within," she said now, beckoning to one of her ladies, handing her the tapestry and her silks. Maybe, she thought, suddenly feeling sad and weighed with years, maybe dear old Katie could have advised her. She'd always said of young John, "He's no a bad bairn, mem, just a gey toom yin. But he'll mend as he grows." Poor Kate. She had not lived to make old bones; yet, perhaps, after all, granted life's hazards and ills, sixty-two years on this earth was not a bad count, when all's said.

"John," Dervorgilla said, turning to her son, "Give me your arm. I feel a touch of stiffness, 'tis the autumn damp."

The boy did as he was bid. Sulky, spoiled, too easily swayed by any hot-head with eloquent speech, his best feature was a genuine love of and respect for his mother.

"Had you good sport?" she asked as they returned to the castle.

"Good enough, but my destrier is too slow! Could you not ask my father to get me a faster mount?"

Dervorgilla shook her head, "Your father has had to give a great deal to the king's coffers during his dispute with the barons. He'd hardly welcome any unnecessary expense this year."

"But mother … you're wealthier than almost any other of the nobility in Britain…nay, in Europe. And I may not ask for one, paltry horse?"

"We may be wealthy, but much of our wealth is spoken for. Great wealth brings great responsibilities, John. Those who have much must give much. It is God's law and only just. Your father and I maintain many charities for the aid of those who cannot help themselves…."

With a moue of distaste, the youngster chimed in, "Yes, all those beggars you feed at the Castle door each day … poor scholars … what good …"

For once his mother spoke with true severity. "John," she said, unconsciously echoing her husband's earlier words, "Do not make yourself appear more foolish and frivolous than necessary."

As they rounded a corner in the path, under the yellowing leaves and scarlet berries of a group of rowans, Ada came towards them, her copper-coloured hair still disordered from her ride, her cheeks glowing.

Mother and daughter kissed fondly.

"Ada, dear one. Ought you to be riding so hard over such difficult ground?"

The girl laughed merrily. "Oh yes, mother. William likes me to be happy while he's busy with his affairs. Besides, I'm a good horsewoman, aren't I, Johnny?"

"Good enough," the boy answered, still sulky.
"But are you not …?"

"No, mother dearest. I'm not 'enceinte' …
yet! What made you think I was?"

"Something Mattie told me yesterday."

Ada coloured. "Mattie's full of wishful
thinking, She wants another bairn in the cradle.
Well, she must wait! Dear knows, you've two
grandchildren already, mother. Won't that do
for a while?"

"One can never have too many bairns."
Dervorgilla's smile was tranquil. "They're the
most precious things we have."

At the doorstep, Alice, grown thin and
somewhat bent with the years, although she was
considerably younger that her mistress, waited.

"The master mason from London's here, my
lady," she said, gently. Alice's voice was always
something of a summer breeze soughing in the
birch-leaves, unlike Katie's rough, hearty tones
had been.

Young John had recovered his spirits.
"Building again, mother?" he chafed.

"Aye, my son. One last memorial to your
father. I plan an Abbey to carry on our ancestor's
great work." Dervorgilla's expression grew
dreamy. "I see a vision of an abbey set under a
great hill, run by the White Monks, in a quiet
valley near the sea."

"Have you chosen the spot, then?" Ada asked,
meanwhile brushing her skirt, where mud had
dried upon its crimson.

"Not finally, but I think the eastern side of Criffell, near Kinderloch, would be the right place. There is no abbey in that part of our domain. It is far enough that travellers coming to and from Dumfries could halt there; the Greyfriars' are often too filled with visitors to have a spare bed. But first I must speak with the mason. Go now and change Ada, for it is almost the dinner hour. John ..." she paused. Would it be wise to say more to this difficult lad? Or should she warn him?

"John," she said, softly, laying a hand on his arm, "Try not to annoy your father. You are ... different, I know. The new generation looks at life with other eyes than our own. But your father is a fine man ... a great man ... and I love him. I love you both. Try to do as he asks. You will come to man's estate soon enough and can decide for yourself how you will live. But, until that time ... do not play with foolishness. You could burn your fingers." The mother leaned forward and kissed her son lovingly while Ada looked on, perplexed.

When Dervorgilla had gone up the winding stone stairs, Ada turned great, curious eyes ... green, like her mother's ... on John.

"What did mother mean ... about burning your fingers?"

John shrugged. "I think she knows that I favour the ideas of de Montfort. He's right. The barons have too much power, too much wealth ..."

"You're crazy, my boy," Ada said airily. "You can never have too much wealth! Wait and see! Why, I thought your chief complaint just now was that we hadn't enough. What about the new horse you said you'd ask father for?"

"That's different," the boy flared. "That's a small, petty thing; I'm speaking of greater matters," he added, pompous and ridiculous.

"Oh, are you, indeed?" Ada mocked. "And who are you, my lord John de Balliol, all of fifteen, scarce even rising sixteen, that you should know so much of 'greater matters'?" She attempted to ruffle her brother's hair, soft and silky.

The boy turned upon her with ferocity. "I do know. I've heard things, Montfort is right. The barons can influence even the king. They can ... can lean upon him and crush even his will. Because, when he needs money, to whom can he turn? Only to them. Then they obtain power over him. It is not right. The king should be absolute!"

"Oh," replied his sister, surveying him knowingly. "I had it wrong then, brother dear. I thought you were against the barons and for Montfort because he promises the peasants a greater measure of independence ... a share of the world's ruling, isn't that what they say?"

"Who cares about the serfs?" John was contemptuous.

"But what's it to you, that the king should be at the Barons' command? You're never likely to be a king, though I'll warrant you'd like that well enough!," she mocked him.

"Of course I'm never likely to be a king," the boy spat out, furious at his sister's taunting. He was silent for a moment. "Unless," ... he said, his eyes growing thoughtful, his mind following a seductive trail ...

"Unless King Alexander dies without further issue? Highly unlikely, my ambitious young hawk. His daughter Margaret is already betrothed to the King of Norway. She's a healthy lass, they say, likely to produce many a bairn in direct line to the throne. Nay, you'll need to be content to be the youngest Balliol."

"And that's good enough for anyone," a gruff voice interrupted them.

Their father's bulk stood between the doorway's light and themselves.

"Come, come, children. It's dinner time, Cease your trifling, wash and groom yourselves. We've a fine troubador to amuse us this evening."

♥ ♥ ♥

John sat at the head of his board. The evening had grown cooler; the wall hangings swayed a little in the draught. It was good to see the logs blaze upon the hearth. His appetite was keen. That was thanks to the good Scots air. In the stews of London's narrow alleys, somehow he never felt himself so fit. If Dervorgilla would hurry, those rich smells from the kitchen quarters could stop tantalising him and begin their rightful business of satisfying a man's belly.

The Lady of Botel's party came into the hall, with Dervorgilla, dressed now in a warmer robe of white wool, embroidered with dark green panels, under a lighter green cloak, leading her daughter and their ladies.

By God' s shirt, but she was a fine woman; she should always wear green.

Green deepened the colour of her beautiful eyes and showed up her delicate skin.

Dervorgilla halted, a few feet in front of the high table and made a deep obeisance to her husband. He stood and bowed, solemnly, courtly as any old-time knight from a romance, his daughter thought, half-smiling, but nevertheless warmed by this old-fashioned, charming love-affair which was so quaintly continued between her parents even now into their old age. She, too, swept a low curtsey to her father before taking her place a little down the table from her mother.

"Mattie," she whispered to the ex-nursemaid who served as her personal maid whenever she visited Botel, and who stood behind her now, waiting to summon the pages with water and clean napkins as they became necessary, "Where is the troubador?"

"Yonder he's, mistress; at the foot of the table, just below the salt."

"What's his song...his new one, I mean?"

"'Tis something about a Frenchie Roland, was't?"

"Oh Mattie, Mattie," Ada giggled. "And you that I've taken with me to France these last two visits!"

Mattie coloured; she'd never yet lost her early unease when the nobility had to be addressed, even although she'd been with Ada since she was a baby. And she hated to be teased. Peasant lass she may have been, aye and would be till she was gone, and none the worse of that; maybe even better than some of these flighty court damsels. But Ada was talking now to her neighbour, Roger, of her de Quincy cousins, spending a night or two on his way to Northumberland, from his native Wigtownshire.

Like her brother, earlier that day, this young man was full of de Montfort and his doings.

"Mark me," he said to Ada now. "There'll be trouble. English Harry's itching for a fight. Your father'll be dragged in."

"Then it'll be the death of him," Ada declared roundly, "Why, Roger, he's an old man. He can no longer do battle. Indeed, I've heard him tell my mother that he dislikes fighting heartily."

Roger de Quincy was a solemn young man. Now he answered Ada, ere he speared a chunk of roast boar.

"No man can afford to dislike fighting when he must fight or lose all he owns."

"All he owns?" Ada opened wide eyes in disbelief.

"Aye. You may think this de Montfort is but a common upstart. But he is gaining powerful friends. And he means to break the Barons' power ..."

"And steal their wealth?" Ada was openly sceptical.

"You'll see. He means business. And your father must oppose him ... or the house of Balliol will die."

"Pooh ... those days are over," Ada said, stretching forth a white hand for the goblet of wine before her. "These are peaceful days. Galloway, all Scotland has never lain so quiet before. Even the Annandales have not harried us this many a day. And for the sake of the marriage between English Harry's daughter and our own King Alex, there's even peace between the two lands north and south of the borderline."

"There's never peace, anywhere, for long," her cousin rejoined obstinately, "That's the way life is. You women may not believe it, but it's so. There's always something...somebody to disturb peace. Peace is not natural," he burst out. "And right now, it's de Montfort who'll disturb things. And your father'll be in the thick of it, just you see."

Their heightened voices caused some of their neighbours at the high table to stare at them. But they were prevented from continuing their argument by Balliol leaving the table, escorting his wife to the centre of the hall, beside the fire, and signalling to the rest of his family to follow suit.

The troubador, thought Ada, following her mother's move slowly, looked uninteresting. His face was chalky white, which seemed odd for a travelling man, and his hair was too yellow and lank. Besides, he looked quite old and his songs would probably be prosy. She was a little sleepy and a little bored, filled with food and good Galloway air. She missed her husband, too. They had grown fond of each other these last few months since their marriage; he was gifted with a witty tongue. He'd have livened things up. At their home they often entertained some of the brighter stars among the younger nobility and the fun was lively. Idly, she seated herself a little away from the group in the middle of the hall. She picked up the collie pup which her father doted on. She laid him in her lap and began to tickle him.

Roger drew near her. "He's a nice pup; should grow into a fine dog."

The puppy snapped as Ada's teasing fingers annoyed him. "He'll need to improve his temper," she said, putting him down on the floor again. "I wish old Tam, mother's terrier, hadn't died. He was almost human."

"Was that the one that lived to be fourteen?"

"Aye. He's buried down by the lilly pond. Young Johnny and I made him a fine headstone. My mother was shocked! She thought us very impious." Ada giggled. The troubador's reedy voice was weaving through the hall now. Just as she'd thought, an ages-old, mile-long tale of ancient French knights killing dragons. She'd heard it all before. .. .and better.

Suddenly, her attention was caught by a tall, swarthy man pushing through the crowd towards her parents.

"It's Hugh!" she exclaimed, leaving her seat and rushing through the crowd of ladies and esquires, servants and castle officials to throw herself into her favourite brother's arms.

"Hello pet," he said, hugging her quickly before he knelt to his mother and father.

Balliol looked alert. "What's amiss, boy? I thought you were dancing at the Edinburgh court?"

"So I was. But we had news four days ago that the Vikings were massing around the Orkney Isles and even now are heading southwest. We've had rumours of this for months past now. I've come to raise a band of Galwegians. We'll ride into Ayrshire ... we think we may hold them there. Would that my grandfather's navy was still in fighting order! Will you come, father?"

John thought for a few moments, deliberating the varying demands likely to be made on him soon.

"No, boy." He shook his great head. "I must to France to Vimeu where a border dispute has broken out. It's best I hold myself ready for that fray. Here there'll be enough Scots, I think, to fight off the Vikings. Their power's coming to an end; they've had their day."

"Hugh," his mother interjected, "Stay awhile,

rest, go fresh tomorrow." Her heart was sad. Was this son, too, to be killed fighting, as Alex had been? He was not even wed yet, let alone leaving an heir to carry on the Balliol name.

"No Mother, thank you but I must make haste. I need go see my groom ... my horse goes lame." He strode from the hall, gathering up a few young knights and grooms as he went. The minstrel resumed his song.

A trifle uneasy on account of the attention which her debate with Roger had drawn, Ada felt she had better make some amends. After all, since her marriage she came to Botel more or less as a guest, and she was conscious that her behaviour could perhaps have given some offence to her mother.

So now she approached Dervorgilla as she began to move towards the side door.

"Mama," she said, using all her winning ways and smiling at her mother. "Let me come and help you."

Dervorgilla finished giving instructions to Alice about the collection of the food which had not been eaten, then she turned responsively to her youngest daughter.

She said, "I should be delighted if you came with me. After all, you're the lady of a great household now and it's right that you should learn to look after your husband's serfs."

Together they put on warm, fur-trimmed pelisses and moved down the flagged passage to the small door at which a few people stood, stamping in the frost of the night to warm their feet, swinging their arms across their chests to keep the blood coursing in their veins.

"There are not many," Ada said, in some surprise.

"No, here there are never many. There are not so many of us in the district, after all!" Dervorgilla said with a wry smile. Looking more serious she added, "It's at Fotheringhay and Kempston that I worry most; in these past ten years there's a vast increase in the villages. In the slack season there's not enough work for them....there I often have twenty or thirty to feed in an evening."

Unthinkingly, Ada said, "Well, when the fight starts between de Montfort and the King, that'll use up some of the men, at least ... and their women'll trail them."

"What are you talking about?"

"Oh, mother. Everyone knows there's going to be a fight. It's bound to come."

"Everyone?"

Ada had the grace to hesitate in her speech. "So many of the young men agree with de Montfort. But the older people ... like father ... they're bound to hate him. And they'll have to fight to stop him for he's the most determined man this country's seen for a long time, Everyone says ..." here Ada broke off, laughing.

Dervorgilla, too, laughed before she turned to watch the young servitors distributing the meat, the good bread, the carcases of fowls, the chunks of fish, remaining from the dinner. Quietly, with dignity, the poor cottars took their food, ducking civilly to their Lady by way of thanks.

"There are few sick or lame," Ada said, frankly assessing the handful of ragged peasants.

"They are mostly healthy enough. Only when the crops are not plentiful do they need extra food. Poor old Jock, from Orchardton's got an old war wound which troubles him sometimes. But there's little I can do save give him a little sweet oil to rub it with."

"Mother, you should have been an Abbess ... you are good with the sick...you love administering affairs ..."

"But then I should not have had my bonny lassies and my brave sons," Dervorgilla said, looking lovingly at this girl's bright face.

They were interrupted by one of the young squires. "Madam," he said, speaking urgently but in a low tone. "My lord sends me to bid you attend him in the hall ... I think ..."

But Dervorgilla did not wait. If John was summoning her, something must be afoot. The quickest way to find out what was to return to her husband.

Chapter Twelve

"My lord?" Dervorgilla said as she approached the seat by the fire where her husband was rising to his feet.

"My lady!" he answered. There was an urgent troubled note in his voice. "Presently a courier arrived from France; things go from bad to worse there. I have decided to leave now." He sighed and Dervorgilla was afraid for him; he looked suddenly an old man, care-worn.

"Will you ride with me? I wish you would, my dear?"

Dervorgilla thought ... perhaps she should go but she had much to do ... the new abbey's plans needed her guiding hand, the monies from Christian's estate must be dealt with ...

"I should dearly love to be with you but ... I fear ... nay, I know I must be here."

John de Balliol nodded his understanding. "I will return as soon as I have settled this dispute ... you take care of affairs here ... and do not vex yourself over this skirmish with the Viking raids ... 'tis naught. Walk with me till I ready myself for my journey." He sighed again. Dervorgilla's heart ached for him ... his shoulders were rounded, now, some of his fire seemed to have left him. She grieved to see him almost visibly ageing.

In their chamber as Balliol ordered his squire to prepare for their long journey, Dervorgilla waited patiently, suggesting clothes to take, discussing with him what needed to be done while he was away. Soon he was ready for departure.

As he left the room he said, "God keep you, my dearling. Take a firm hand with young John. I will be home as soon as I possibly may be. And remember me in your prayers, as I shall remember you." He turned and gave her a long embrace, kissing her on the mouth. "And remember too, that I love you always, with all my heart. God be with you." And then he was gone.

Forlornly, Dervorgilla roamed about the room to be interrupted by Hugh's entry. "Mother, I cannot ride tonight ... my horse needs attention"

"Oh, I'm glad," she replied. "Will you send a servant to find your sister, there is something I have to speak with both of you about."

Ada was soon found. "Mother, do not be so disturbed. Father will return soon."

"Yes, dear, I trust in God that it will be so. But, while both you and Hugh are here I want to tell you what I have already dictated to my clerk of the law. I think you should know ... and remember ... my wishes ... nay, my registered orders in the event of your father dying before long ..."

She raised a hand to check Ada's quick intervening. She sighed and looked seriously at her children.

"If ... <u>when</u> he dies, which being so much older than I ... I wish his heart to be taken from his body by the surgeon, for it to be embalmed and then placed within a casket of ivory, this then to be banded with silver. This shall be beside me where 'ere I go." Ada began to weep and Hugh coughed and shuffled his feet.

"Mother," he said. "Do not let us speak of ..."

"Yes, Hugh, we must. Your father has gone into a disputatious situation. You, yourself may be about to do the same. Now is a very good time for you to learn what lies ahead. My new abbey, beside the Solway Firth at Kinderloch will be ready ..." she smiled gently ... "before, I hope, I myself shall leave this world. When I do, I have decreed, and my clerk of the law has so recorded it; I wish my body to be buried there near the high altar."

She straightened her back and looked commandingly at her children.

"I also wish your father's heart, in its casket, to be laid to rest upon my bosom, so that our two hearts may be together. This shall be our resting place for all time"

There was silence.

Dervorgilla was fighting the tears which were filling her eyes;

Ada was sobbing quietly. "It shall be as you wish, mother" she began when Dervorgilla interrupted her ...

"One more thing children. While I shall live, your father's heart ... 'my sweet, silent companion', shall be placed at the high table beside me, as if it were he, himself, present. To it, every course of every meal shall be served; this said food being, at the end of every meal, distributed in full to those indigents who await my charity at the doors of whichever place I shall be at. I also ask that the bidding prayer be said at our new house of learning beside the village of Oxford, honouring your father's memory. Both there and in our new Galloway Abbey, prayers shall be said daily for the souls of your father and myself. Do you understand?"

The young man and his sister nodded. It was hard for them to speak until Hugh mumbled, "Mother, dearest and best of mothers, all shall be ordered exactly as you say."

Ada intervened, "You look so sad, you are tired now ... may I call your chamber maid to disrobe you and ..."

Her mother interrupted her. "Ada, my dear, dear, girl, you are wrong; truly I am tired; but I am only a very little sad. What must be has to be ... death is as nothing compared to the happiness your father and I shared through our life together." She smiled, looked into the fire's dying embers before continuing.

"I think perhaps you know I was not entirely a willing bride to a stranger knight so much older than I, but we came to enjoy a true and deep love. More than that no human being may ask. With God's help our union has been a truly blessed one. And I am content." Dervorgilla paused, lost in her thoughts.

Hugh broke the silence. "Mother, you saw, as I did, that my father looked weary ... older." He hesitated, not wanting to hurt his mother in any way. "If ... God forfend ... if anything untoward should happen to him in France, who knows ..." he stumbled again over his words ... "who can order these affairs?"

Dervorgilla smiled at her son, "His chief squire Sir Cecil will, he has been instructed by me."

"You are not to worry Mother dear. This is far ahead," Hugh said, "My father is yet strong enough for all the years he carries."

"Pray God that it may be so, but these things must be ordered and I am comforted that you children should know what has to be done. Now, leave me and sleep safely and well."

She kissed Ada and Hugh. There was no need of further words.

♥ ♥ ♥

Winter was dragging its comfortless days to an end; the snowdrops were lying like animated snowflakes across the river verges and the meadows. Dervorgilla and Hugh sat in a small withdrawing chamber by a log fire.

"Thankfully," Hugh was saying, "we've seen the last of these Viking encroachments; their lust to conquer our land seems to have weakened. I think they will no longer trouble us ... but we have fresh concerns; my cousin Comyn ... your sister's son, is brewing mischief I hear ... I wish my father was safe home again."

"Indeed," Dervorgilla began when her youngest child, John, came into the room, flinging the door wide; he bowed sketchily to his mother, acknowledged his brother with a tilt of the head.

Impetuously he tumbled out his words. "Mother," he said, "is there yet no news of father's return from Vimeu? I fain would speak with him on matters of state."

"Matters of state?" Hugh taunted his young brother. "You are grown mighty important are you now?"

"And wherefore not? I am a Balliol. Our claim to the throne of Scotland may be less tenuous than we might believe ... and I for one shall not wait for my chance ..."

"Your chance? You, the youngest of our line? By God, brother, you strut too like a peacock for my taste!" Hugh's temper was rising.

John flung back at him ... his colour flushing, his temper scarcely held in check "You may be a scholar and a contemplative ... I am a man of action!"

Even as John approached his brother menacingly there was a knock on the door. Hugh opened the door. A sombre faced Sir Cecil moved forward and knelt before Dervorgilla.

"My lady, madam," he said ... Dervorgilla interrupted him, rising swiftly to her feet, her hand going to her heart ...

"Sir Cecil," she said firmly. "You bring ill news?" The colour was draining from her face and her hands began to tremble. "It is my husband? What ...? Is ...?"

Hugh and John were standing, silent. Only the crumbling of a log on the fire sounded through the chamber. Like a knell of death, Dervorgilla thought as Sir Cecil bowed his head.

"My dear Lord Balliol died three days hence. His heart failed him ... of a sudden. He had concluded his business the day before and was in a high state of eagerness to start for home, but ..." the man's voice faltered, "'twas ordered otherwise." Sir Cecil paused, then said gently, "I have Baron Balliol's body, my lady. It has been lain by my men in the family chapel and Brother Timothy even now prays for his soul ... but I believe his remains are destined for Barnard Castle after his heart has been embalmed?" Dervorgilla bowed her head in assent.

"I must go to the chapel." Dervorgilla said, quietly. Hugh laid his hand on her arm. "First, mother, tell me what I should do to aid you?"

Sir Cecil interrupted. "Let me do aught that I can for your aid and comfort, My Lady ..."

Dervorgilla said, "I thank you, Sir Cecil. But you have journeyed long and must be weary. Take care of yourself and your retainers. My sons will be my aides. Go now ... rest ... and my deepest gratitude goes with you."

As Sir Cecil left the room, John muttered, "Here's a pretty state!"

Hugh glared at him. For a moment it seemed as if their earlier dispute might flare afresh, but John sat down heavily upon a bench, chewing his thumb and was silent.

"Hugh," Dervorgilla said. "Please send for Brother Matthew ... he is skilled in medicine and he knows the surgeons well. We must find such a one who will take your father's heart and embalm it ..." Hugh nodded his agreement. "Then send my silversmith to me. I will instruct him to make a fitting casket ..." Dervorgilla paused. With tears beginning to flow, she said. "Thus will your dear father's heart accompany me wherever I shall go; and when my own time to die comes, be sure I am laid in my new abbey on Solway-side with the casket resting upon my own heart."

Through her tears Dervorgilla smiled at her sons. "I fancy, through time, that sacred building might come to be known as 'The Abbey of the Sweethearts'."

♥ ♥ ♥

And so it came to be that Dervorgilla's new abbey, built by the Cistercians, under the shadow of Criffel Hill, did indeed become known as "Dulce Cor" ... the Latin for "Sweetheart Abbey"